FOX

INDIGORIVER
PUBLISHING

S.R.W. BLACK

Fox: A Southern Fairy Tail

Editors: Noëlla Simmons, Stephanie Thompson
Cover and Interior Design: Emma Elzinga

Indigo River Publishing

3 West Garden Street, Ste. 718
Pensacola, FL 32502
www.indigoriverpublishing.com

Ordering Information:

Quantity Sales: Special discounts are available on quantity purchases by corporations, associations, and others. For details, contact the publisher at the address above.

Orders by US trade bookstores and wholesalers: Please contact the publisher at the address above.

Printed in the United States of America

Library of Congress Control Number: 2024912495
ISBN: 978-1-964686-00-4 (paperback)   978-1-964686-01-1 (ebook)

First Edition

For Stephen

Contents

Chapter 1

THE STORY WITHIN A STORY

In the past, around the turn of the century, there lived a family of foxes in the rural community of Big Creek, Alabama, outside of Mobile. In truth, many foxes lived there, and they were all related to each other in some way or another, be it second cousins or third aunts or what have you, but for the purpose of this story we shall discuss one particular fox family living on the outskirts of Farmer Reynolds's property.

Farmer Reynolds owned 175 acres of fertile land near the primeval forest that flourished alongside the Escatawpa River. He had chickens, three cows, two pigs, a black Labrador retriever named Tomboy, and a calico cat named Ruby. The foxes made their den in a fallen tree, where Farmer Reynolds's dove hunting meadow met the deep woods on the southeast side of his property. Today, more houses and fewer trees appear along the southern landscape, but years ago, when the age was not quite as modern as now, this fox family had miles of woods to roam through unfettered.

And so, our story begins on a cloudy morning in early June, just as dawn is breaking through the pines towering like massive hairy skeletons in the foggy light. Beneath the pines rests a fallen tree—the oldest and biggest among them. Its broken trunk has created a natural fort, under which our family has built a fine den deep in the red earth. As the ghostly fog rolls in and waves over the meadow that lies adjacent to the forest, we spy a flame-colored fox trotting steadily across the field to the opening of the den. He is the patriarch of the family, and his given name is Pennyroyal. Pennyroyal carries a large rabbit in his mouth. As he descends quietly into the dark tunnel below the fallen tree, he drops the rabbit abruptly and growls at the three kits rolling about the den.

"Stop all this roughhousing! Where is your mother? Stop, I say!"

Chastened, the kits stop their play and observe their father. As foxes go, he is quite large, and just now, his countenance is imposing in the confines of the den. The kits observe him with a mixture of affection and fear. Pennyroyal is decidedly unamused by the kits. Their names are as follows: Marigold, a lovely little girl fox with a white stripe on her forehead; Cricket, another girl, who is quite small and delicate looking; and Shadow, a boy fox whom Pennyroyal regards stonily and who returns his father's stare sheepishly.

The den is one large room with the fallen tree as a roof. The earth is warm and patted dry within. It has a main opening that faces the meadow and a smaller opening at the back facing the woods that the kits can barely squeeze through.

Just then, a beautiful adult fox with a white stripe above her eyes enters the den. She is carrying a dead mouse in her mouth and drops it where the rabbit lay at Pennyroyal's feet.

"Mama! Mama!" the kits cry, pouncing on their mother joyfully. She indulges them with licks and nuzzles, and, turning to Pennyroyal, gives him a wet lick right on the snout. The two meet each other's gaze, and Pennyroyal's eyes soften.

"Ah, Moon, what a lovely mouse you have brought!" Pennyroyal sighs happily at his mate and ignores the kits, who have forgotten their parents and are now fighting over the rabbit. Marigold pushes Shadow, who has the rabbit clumsily between his jaws. He drops the rabbit, and in a rage of fiery fur pounces on Marigold, who kicks him off with her hind legs. Shadow's eyes burn with startled anger. He flies at his sister again, and the two tumble to-and-fro along the den, the rabbit utterly forgotten. Cricket watches the spectacle lazily from her mother's side.

"All right you two. Quiet, quiet," Moon coaxes, stealthily grabbing Shadow's tail with her forepaw to stop a frontal attack. "There is enough for everyone."

Shadow and Marigold eye each other suspiciously as the family gathers around for the feast, then quickly forget their grievances as Pennyroyal allocates each their supper. Everyone dives in hungrily, save Cricket, who is content nursing from Moon.

As supper ends, the fox kits curl up next to their mother, with Pennyroyal standing sentry at the mouth of the den.

"Mama, tell us a story," Cricket yawns.

"Yes, Mama. Please tell us a story." Marigold and Shadow chime in unison, their eyes fixed on Moon's kindly face.

"All right, my dear ones. I will tell you a story about First Fox, who is our ancestor. When the world began, the Great Creator fashioned First Fox out of lightning and the red earth you see around you. First Fox burned bright. He was handsome, quick, and the cleverest of all animals. The Great Creator was pleased with his creation and gave First Fox the power of the sun in his tail. In the winter months, First Fox had but to wave his fiery tail and any creature that had succumbed to the cold would be instantly warmed, even to the point of bringing them back to life. And again, with one wave of his tail, plants would grow, producing plentiful food to eat. In this way, First Fox was the caretaker of all creation.

"One day, during high summer, First Fox was walking through the cornfields First Man had planted. There had been too much rain, and the corn had drowned and failed to grow. First Man approached First Fox and asked him to please use his magic tail to make the corn grow. He told First Fox that his family depended on the corn to eat, and without it, they would die. So, First Fox ran quicker than lightning through the fields, warming the corn with his fiery tail. The corn began to grow, and First Man thanked First Fox for saving him.

"Later, the world turned cold and all the animals, save First Fox, retreated into their hideaways to await the coming spring. But because First Fox had the power of the sun in his bushy tail, he walked along as though the cold did not exist. Just then, First Man came speeding up to First Fox.

"'Please,' said First Man, 'my daughter is dying of cold. Please come and save her with your burning tail.'

"But First Fox saw the opportunity to be sly. He had seen First Man's daughter and knew that she was very beautiful. She could also sing enchanting songs.

"'I will save your daughter, but you must give her

to me to be my wife. She is the only one who is as beautiful as I am. Together we will be more beautiful than the sun.'

"But First Man did not wish his daughter to belong to the arrogant fox. So, he devised a plan to fool First Fox for the Great Creator made the fox the cleverest of all animals, but man is cleverer still.

"'Give me seven days to prepare her for you,' said First Man. 'But please, come and save her now! She is dying and will be of no use to anyone if you delay. After seven days, I will deliver my daughter to you, and she will be yours.'

"First Fox agreed to First Man's conditions, and hastened to the daughter, who lay dying of cold upon her bed. Indeed, she was already dead when they arrived. First Fox regarded the beautiful creature, and thinking of First Man's promise, waved his fiery tail over the girl's body. Immediately, she began to draw breath, and the blue cold that had claimed her melted away, and her flesh turned rosy and warm. Her eyes fluttered, and as the miracle of life poured into her newly beating heart, she began to sing.

Fire has touched me,
Of fire I am born.
Though I die at night,
I am resurrected with the dawn.

"First Man thanked First Fox for saving his beloved daughter and again promised to deliver her to First Fox after seven days time. But as First Fox walked away, First Man took up his axe and went to the forest. There, he found the loveliest tree and chopped it down. Then, First Man began to fashion a wooden girl out of the trunk of the tree. As he worked, the block of wood came to look exactly like his own dear daughter, whom First Fox had saved, but with whom he could not part. After seven days, First Man came to First Fox, carrying the wooden daughter in his arms.

"'Here is my daughter, as I promised you.' And he set the wooden sculpture down before First Fox.

"Now, since the wooden girl was so cunningly made, First Fox did not realize First Man had tricked him. He regarded the sculpture with admiration.

"'Please,' said First Fox to the wooden girl, 'sing a song to me.'

"But the wooden girl remained silent.

"'Tell me a story then about your people, so that I may contemplate the ways of men.'

"The wooden daughter made no reply.

"'Why are you silent? Are you dying of cold again?' And First Fox felt the wooden girl's arm, and indeed it felt both hard and cold.

"'Here now, I will warm you with my tail so that you may sing to me with gratitude.' And First

Fox covered the little wooden statue with his burning tail. But instead of the girl reviving to life, the wood cracked and splintered from the heat. And then First Fox realized that he had been fooled by First Man, and the girl he saw before him was only a block of wood.

"First Fox burned with anger and vowed revenge upon First Man. That night, as the moon rose high in the sky, First Fox ran like lightning between the rows of First Man's crops, setting them all ablaze. The fire raged all night, until nothing was left of the crops First Man had so carefully planted.

"No one saw First Fox do this terrible deed. No one—that is, except the Great Creator who lives in the sky.

"That night, the Great Creator came to First Fox in a dream.

"'What have you done, First Fox? For what reason have you done this evil thing?'

"First Fox could make no reply, for he was ashamed. Instead, he bowed his head and pawed the ground fretfully.

"'Because you have proven yourself wicked, I am taking back your magic. No longer will you be able to harness the power of the sun with your tail. You will be forced to hunt for your food, and it will run from you. And you will see your death, and nothing will be able to bring you back. But because First Man has deceived you and caused you to do evil, I will punish him by giving you his daughter after all. Never again will she return to the company of men, and because her father has dealt with you so treacherously with the wooden girl, he will not recognize his own daughter.'

"The Great Creator then rose on his jeweled wings into the night sky and faded into starlight. First Fox awoke from the dream and saw that dawn was rising. And there beside him slept the most beautiful vixen he had ever seen. Her red fur glimmered in the morning rays, and her black paws were delicately formed. She awoke, and the two foxes regarded one another in silence for a long time.

"First Fox finally spoke. 'You are mine,' he said solemnly.

"'I am yours,' the vixen replied. Her eyes were beautiful and sad.

"The two rose together, and side by side, retreated into the Great Forest that surrounded them."

Moon pauses her storytelling and watches the kits' breath evenly rise and fall as they dream. Sighing deeply, and with satisfaction, she lays her head sweetly upon the earth, and sleeps.

Chapter 2

WHAT LURKS IN THE FOREST

"Come on, Mistletoe. I want to go!" Shadow cries out to the gangly fox who has arrived at the den to discuss hunting with Pennyroyal. Mistletoe is Shadow's older brother, from last year's litter, and has been on his own for a few months now. He is almost full grown, but still a bit long in the legs, like a gawky teenager who has not quite filled out yet. Despite his awkwardness, he looks remarkably like Pennyroyal. Mistletoe is adjusting well to being on his own, although he still visits his parents' den regularly to ask for advice and for companionship, for he is a bit lonely after the tumble and bumble of being a kit.

"Come ooon, Mistletoe. Pleeeaase?" Shadow nags his older brother, who to him is even more spectacular than their father. "I can go hunting with you and help you catch a rabbit!"

Mistletoe pauses in his conversation with his father and turns to his little brother, who is wagging his little tail vigorously and watching him excitedly.

"Take him with you," instructs Pennyroyal gruffly. "He needs to learn to hunt, but he will just slow me down. I have a family to feed, and you have only yourself." And with that, Pennyroyal turns abruptly and escapes back down the den. Mistletoe arches his brow slightly, but he is used to his father's rough personality. He contemplates Shadow, who is now grinning unabashedly at him.

"Come on, half-pint. Let's go." And the two foxes start off together into the field outside the den. Mistletoe races along in front, with Shadow behind imitating his brother's effortlessly slouched posture.

They sprint along this way for a minute or so. After reaching tall grass that conceals the two foxes, Mistletoe slows to a trot, allowing Shadow to come up beside him. Mistletoe turns his head and smiles kindly at his younger brother.

"Did you know that a long time ago, the dam the men built at Big Creek Lake wasn't there, and there was no lake?" Mistletoe's eyes glitter as he speaks. "And the land Farmer Reynolds owns, well, there used to be people, whose skin was black, who lived on the land called sharecroppers. They lived out in the woods and gave a portion of their crops to the man who owned the land, and he let them stay there." Truthfully, Mistletoe has just learned these facts from the other animals he has met out on his own, namely Maw Maw and Paw Paw, the gopher tortoises who live in the field over and are the oldest living creatures the animals know. But he likes the look of wonder on Shadow's face, and so he tells him about the history of the land on which they dwelt with an air of greater wisdom than he possesses. The two walk on in this way for some time, but when Mistletoe exhausts his store of interesting tales to report, he deftly turns the conversation to Shadow.

"How are things at home?" he asks his little brother, who is moving briskly to keep up.

"Oh, fine. Cricket gets all the attention, and Marigold is a snitch. Just the other day, I had left the den when Mama said not to and found a patch of blueberries. I was going to give some to Cricket, and even to Marigold, if they kept quiet, but Marigold said she wouldn't and that she was going to tell Mama. Which she did, and I got in trouble and wasn't allowed to leave the den to go with Mama later to practice hunting. But at least Mama didn't tell Papa. She said that not getting to pretend hunt was punishment enough. But I promised myself I'm going to get Marigold back—"

Just then, Francis, the raven, flies on midnight wings over the pair and descends to the ground before the brothers, interrupting their conversation. He flutters his wings nervously, alert as a sentinel.

"Farmer Reynolds is in the field hunting doves, gentle foxes. Find better cover than this." Francis is a friend to the animals on the farmer's property. He eats alongside the chickens, picking up his news from them and his daily patrols over field and forest. Mrs. Reynolds named him after the saint who was so friendly with all the animals; even Tomboy and Ruby leave him alone. He can understand human language and occasionally breaks into poetry without warning. All in all, Francis is a very smart bird. But today, he is all business with the foxes.

Mistletoe pauses for the briefest moment, then turning to Shadow whispers, "All right, Shadow, this way. Follow my lead." He slinks low to the ground, his black paws moving soundlessly over the earth. The two weave their way through the tall grass until they reach the edge of the forest. Before them lays about a yard of open clover between the grass and the trees. "Let me go first," he whispers over his shoulder to Shadow, who watches him with wide eyes. Slowly, and with an air of nonchalance, Mistletoe skulks across the clover and into the forest. Just before he disappears into the deepening shadows, he turns and soundlessly beckons Shadow across. The younger fox imitates his brother, his body slouchy and his step light but determined. Just as he is about to reach the trees for cover, a shot rings out behind him, and a frenzied flock of birds rises into the dying light. Shadow's body shudders involuntarily as he scampers toward Mistletoe, all effects of composure lost.

"Come on," Mistletoe says evenly, and trots deeper into the protective foliage. Shadow follows obediently, and the two foxes weave their way over roots and around bushes. The moon is rising and growing brighter in the falling dusk, and the woods are dark and safe within.

They walk on for some time. Deep in the forest, the trees grow more thickly together, and the path Mistletoe follows seems to disappear before them. A wind has kicked up, and the tops of the trees sway, their leaves rustling eerily.

"Where are we going?" Shadow asks, with just a hint of quiver in his voice. Before Mistletoe can reply, an owl hoots close by overhead, and the sound of great wings mounting the night air chills them to the bone. The two cross over a small stream that has flooded the path Mistletoe is intuitively following.

"This water is made by something called an artesian well," Mistletoe orates as they splash through the muddy water. "It's a fountain that never dries up."

For all the world, Mistletoe acts as though he knows exactly where he is going. As they travel, they come to a makeshift pen with two wild boars inside of it.

"Hello there!" Mistletoe utters softly to the boars.

"Hello. We have been caught by the farmer. We know he means to eat us!" The boars gaze back at the foxes mournfully. On this bright evening, the moon is full, the sparkling light peeking through the tops of the trees. The foxes' eyes shine in the darkness, their senses sharpening. The wind has begun to howl, although the air is warm with the Alabama June heat.

"What will you do if we free you?" Mistletoe asks suspiciously. Earlier that year while hunting, a wild boar had chased him.

"Why, we will eat you!" And the boars laugh sardonically despite their sad confinement. Mistletoe and Shadow back away from the pen, circling round it to regain the path. They can still hear the boars laughing, awaiting their death, as the brothers stumble through the undergrowth, which has grown very heavy.

"Do you know where we're going?" asks Shadow nervously. He has never been this far from the den before, and the deepening shadows of the forest move and tremble like dark creatures in the night.

"Keep following me," instructs Mistletoe calmly. "I smell a rabbit. We'll have a nice supper to bring back home."

The foxes suddenly find themselves in a small clearing in the presence of an old, gnarled oak tree, dead and twisted with age. The moon rises overhead, lighting the tree as if by magic in silvery light. A strange vine or rope with something that looks like a human head made of wood hangs down from one of the tree's branches.

Mistletoe squints his eyes as he examines the odd growth, sniffing the air as he does. "Why, that looks like a face!"

"Where are we?" squeaks Shadow, who is making no effort to disguise his nervousness. The tree has an ominous feel, and the weird vine-head-thing really does look like a face. There's the outline of a mouth, indents for a nose, and the eyes—

Without warning, the eyes on the face open, and the vine turns so it can regard the two creatures who have disturbed its slumber. The foxes' own eyes widen with fear. As the wooden head fixes its gaze upon them, the trunk of the tree grinds and creaks. With a deafening crack, the trunk shudders and opens, revealing a space within swirling with darkness. The two foxes cry out in terror. The wind, which has lulled since Mistletoe and Shadow approached the strange oak, screams through the forest, and a strong, unseen force pulls them toward the opening in the tree.

"Mistletoe, help!" shrieks Shadow as the two are

pulled closer to the gaping hole, the evil eyes of the wooden head fixated on them.

Suddenly, a great brown stag appears in the clearing directly behind the foxes. He stamps his large hooves loudly, tossing his great antlered head about—the look in his eyes wild. "Run!" he shouts, and as abruptly as he appeared, he bounds off into the forest.

"Run, Shadow! Run!" Mistletoe yells to his brother. Immediately, as though the spell transfixing them has broken, the foxes hurry in the direction the stag took, leaving the tree and its swirling darkness behind them.

"Keep running!" Mistletoe urges on. The pair splash through the puddle made by the artesian well, stumbling over roots and undergrowth as they retrace their path through the woods.

"Why are you running?" shout the boars as the foxes race past their pen frantically. "Is something chasing you?" Their mocking laughter rings in the foxes' ears. Ahead, at the edge of the forest, stands the stag, silhouetted in moonlight. As the brothers speed toward him, he turns, leaping into the field. Just as the foxes reach the tree line, a shot rings out, and the stag abruptly disappears into the starry night. The two brothers bolt as fast as they can through the tall grass, almost forgetting each other in the rush to reach the fox den. Finally, after what seems an endless ordeal, they gain the entrance to the den, tumbling down the open tunnel in a flurry of fur and fear.

Moon looks up abruptly from where she sits, nursing both Cricket and Marigold. Her face changes from a look of bemusement to bewilderment as her two sons stop short of slamming into her, panting and exchanging wild glances.

"Did the rabbits get the better of you this time, Mistletoe?" she asks, looking at her older son with growing perturbation. Pennyroyal has not returned to the den yet, and Moon is growing hungry.

"I'm sorry, Mother," whimpers Mistletoe, catching his breath. "Something happened in the woods, and Farmer Reynolds was out hunting. We barely made it out," he cries, shuddering as he looks at Shadow, who has collapsed on the ground, panting and quivering.

Moon's eyes narrow almost to a close as her silence beckons Mistletoe to tell her the story of their grand adventure, which has resulted in no food for dinner.

"We were walking along, and Francis came and told us that Farmer Reynolds was hunting doves in the field. So, we went into the forest for cover. We were walking along just fine and dandy—we passed the artesian well—and then we came upon a part of the woods I've never been in before. There was this old tree, and as we approached it, it came alive and tried to pull us into its trunk. A giant stag appeared and told us to leave. So we did. We ran back the way we came, following the stag. Just as he reached the field, we heard a gun fire, and the stag disappeared. I don't know if he was shot. I didn't see him fall. One minute he was there, and the next, he was gone. We ran all the way here." As Mistletoe finishes the story, he bows his head low, remembering his ordeal. Marigold and Cricket are speechless, their eyes wide with amazement.

"I see," intones Moon evenly. "And who is this savior stag, pray tell?"

"I don't know. I've never seen him before."

Mistletoe raises his head slightly, meeting his mother's gaze. As she examines him, she acknowledges to herself that there is no falsehood in his face. Softening, she pats over to Shadow, who is still lying on the ground in a state of shock, and wraps her body around him. He nuzzles into her warm belly, and nurses soundlessly, his eyes closed. Moon licks his muzzle gently. Then turning back to Mistletoe, she says, "Stay here for the evening, Mistletoe. Your father will be home soon, and we will all share a meal together."

"But Mother, have you ever heard about a tree doing that? Or the stag; do you know him?" Mistletoe lays down at Moon's feet, just like a young kit.

Marigold and Cricket shuffle over to their mother and nurse alongside Shadow. The three of them growl and push softly at each other.

"I have never heard of a tree doing that. But my father used to say that the spirits of dead men from long ago roam the haunted woods with their witchcraft. Pennyroyal may know the stag you saw. We shall ask him when he returns."

And as though he were waiting to be beckoned, at that very moment, Pennyroyal arrives, with several mice between his jaws. Dropping them before Moon and the kits, he turns to Mistletoe sternly.

"What's this? Out all night hunting and nothing to show for it? Or just fooling around with your younger brother?"

"Wait a moment," cautions Moon. "Mistletoe has something he wants to tell you." And nodding her head toward her older son, Mistletoe retells the whole story of the tree, the stag, and Farmer Reynolds to his father.

"Do you know this stag? Or the tree?" Moon asks her mate.

"I have never seen this tree of which you speak, but from now on, you will stay away from that part of the forest," instructs Pennyroyal. "As for the stag, I may know him, but a long time has passed since we have spoken." Pennyroyal allows his voice to trail off into silence, indicating that the conversation is over. After a moment, he divides up dinner for Moon, the kits, and Mistletoe, who gets the last of the spoils.

"I'll make sure Shadow does what he's supposed to," announces Marigold pertly. Shadow groans, and catching Mistletoe's attention, rolls his eyes dramatically, mocking Marigold wordlessly behind her back. Chastened by Pennyroyal, Mistletoe turns his attention to his paws, pretending to find something very interesting there. As the sun lightens the sky outside the den, Mistletoe squeezes himself into the darkest part of the den and dozes off.

Chapter 3

VICIOUS VISITORS

Mistletoe stayed with his parents and siblings for the next three days, finding solace in the familiar routine of a kit (although he is really too old to play the part for very much longer). Still, the time spent with his family has brought him comfort, and the incident with the tree and the stag have largely been forgotten. On the morning of the third day, just before dawn wakes from her slumber and stretches herself across the sky, Mistletoe, Shadow, and Cricket have decided to play a prank on Marigold. She's been nearly unbearable since the brothers arrived together at the den brimming with confusion and fear. Appointing herself the mother when Moon is out hunting, Marigold has been guarding the mouth of the den as though all creation depends upon her vigilance. For the most part, this has played out without too much bickering—Shadow and Mistletoe have been content to bide their time until the next adventure, and Cricket hardly ever ventures outside anyway—but everyone has their limit, even foxes, and the brothers have finally decided to pay Marigold back in kind.

"Okay, Cricket," whispers Mistletoe. "Marigold is taking a nap. Sneak past her and go sit outside and start whimpering. Make a good show of it now. Shadow, you scamper out the back way and stand on the broken tree over the den. Wait for my signal. Does everyone know what they're supposed to do?"

"Yes!" whisper the two kits in unison excitedly, their eyes gleaming in the darkness of the den.

"Shhhh. Be very quiet," instructs Mistletoe, nodding to Cricket. She slowly makes her way up the opening of the den, stepping lightly with her small feet past Marigold, who is snoring loudly in the dead center of the den's opening. Cricket weaves her way soundlessly past her, and emerging from the den, lies down next to a rock a little ways away. As she moves stealthily past her sister, Shadow clambers out the very small opening at the back of the den. He tries to move as quietly as Cricket, but instead finally squeezes himself through noisily. Mistletoe grimaces slightly at his brother's clumsiness but doesn't move a muscle. The sound of Shadow's exit has roused Marigold, but as she rolls over, she lets out a tremendous yawn and starts snoring again peacefully. At this moment, a sad whimpering can be heard from beyond the entrance to the den. Marigold wakes abruptly mid-snore, and shaking the sleep from her eyes, peers into the den. Mistletoe pretends to sleep in the corner, but the two younger foxes are missing. Alarmed, and because the whimpering has grown louder to an all-out wail, Marigold's eyes grow frantic, and she exits the den in search of her siblings.

"Cricket? Cricket! What's the matter? Are you hurt?" Marigold rushes to her sister, who is rolling to and fro as though in the worst straits of agony. As Marigold attempts to coax a comprehensible response from the dramatic Cricket, Mistletoe skulks behind the two without attracting Marigold's attention. Smoothly and quietly, he locates a fallen branch and drags it across the mouth of the den, blocking the entrance. As he pulls the dead branch into place, Cricket's cries turn into screams. Desperate, Marigold grabs hold of her sister's tail, attempting to drag her back into the safety of the den.

"Shadow, now!" yells Mistletoe at the top of his lungs. Puzzled, Marigold drops Cricket's tail just as Shadow leaps from the roof of the den onto his unsuspecting, annoying sister. He grabs a hold of her ear with his jaws and flips her over onto her back, pinning her there with his forelegs. Marigold's paws scrabble in the dirt, and finally making purchase, she kicks Shadow off and attempts to flee into the den. However, the dead branch effectively blocks her progress, and as she scrambles to fly off in another direction, Mistletoe pounces on her from behind, playfully batting her back and forth as Shadow again leaps onto her gyrating back.

"Go, Shadow and Mistletoe, go!" shouts Cricket gleefully, utterly amused by her brothers' antics.

As the foxes play, Pennyroyal appears on the fallen tree that makes the roof of the den. His look is so severe that without words, the fight dissipates, and the younger animals quietly align themselves in a semicircle on the ground below their father. His voice is clear and grave.

"I was out hunting. I had almost caught the rabbit I'd been chasing all night, when Francis flew at me and distracted me before I reached my prey. He said that he saw a pack of coyotes circling Farmer Reynolds's house and barn." The kits exchange looks of alarm with one another. Only Mistletoe remains fixated on his father, his ears very alert. Shadow notices his older brother's composure and mimics it.

Pennyroyal continues solemnly, "Just after Francis flew off, a very large one-eyed coyote approached me. He said his name is Thorn, and that he and his family have traveled here from Louisiana. He said that just yesterday, they were in a burnt-out suburb in Mississippi called Hurley." Pennyroyal paused. "Thorn said they were traveling through the area when what they saw here was good." The leader of the foxes eyes each of his children seriously. None of them return his gaze.

"He also said that if we do not interfere in their business, they will share the spoils of the land with us."

"What did you say, Father?" Mistletoe has forgotten the part he played in the kits' silly game and instead intensely focuses on Pennyroyal.

Pennyroyal regards his children. "You are aware of the treaty we have with Tomboy and Ruby, Farmer Reynolds's dog and cat. We do not touch their chickens, and they will lead a hunt away from us and the den. We have also always shared information back and forth between us.

"Years ago, when your mother and I moved to this property, Farmer Reynolds had a terrible mice problem in his field. Tomboy and Ruby were unable to keep up with it. They asked us to help them get rid of the mice. If we could do that, and as long as we did not poach the chickens, they would never intentionally put us in harm's way. They also promised to share information from the farm with us, so we would know where to hunt so as not to disturb the farmer's crops.

"We have kept our part of the treaty, as have they. But Thorn wants the chickens. I told him about the treaty we have with Farmer Reynolds's animals, and he said that if we informed Tomboy or Ruby of their presence, they would surely attack us and take our territory by force.

"I want no part of this business, but I cannot afford to lose our den or hunting grounds. I told Thorn that we could not go against our treaty with the farmer's animals. If they did not attack the chickens, then we would not interfere with them. Thorn simply laughed. As he laughed, another large coyote, this one female, emerged from the surrounding trees. She had the rabbit I had been tracking in her teeth, and she was flanked by another coyote, her and Thorn's pup I think, but he was almost grown, and nearly as large as his parents. I had not seen or heard them until they emerged from the shadows.

"Thorn said nothing more but continued laughing. As he laughed, the gang of coyotes walked into the darkness of the forest. I watched them until they disappeared, and then I ran here. I need to speak to your mother. Is she back from the hunt yet?" Pennyroyal's eyes dart around in search of Moon, betraying the anxiety he must have felt with the coyotes. The younger foxes sense his apprehension and look around frantically for their mother. Dawn has risen with glowing arms into the sky, lighting everything in her path. Still, no sign of Moon.

"Into the den, all of you!" commands Pennyroyal, collecting himself. The kits and Mistletoe obey without question. Mistletoe silently moves the branch away from the tunnel, and together all the foxes file into the den beneath the fallen tree.

Inside, Cricket trembles with fright. "Where's Mama? Where's my Mama?" She whimpers against Marigold, who attempts to comfort her sister, her own eyes welling with emotion. Mistletoe sits down at the head of the tunnel, his head erect, and stares out the mouth of the den, hoping to catch sight of Moon returning. Shadow stands beside his brother, imitating his alert posture. Pennyroyal is pacing the belly of the den wordlessly, casting a glance toward Mistletoe every few minutes, hoping to see his mate.

After an hour of anxious waiting, Mistletoe loudly whispers, "She's here!" Across the meadow, Moon's flame-colored body darts in and out of the tall grass. She treads stealthily, staying close to the edge of the forest as she makes her way to the den and her family. Within minutes, she skirts past Mistletoe and Shadow down the opening tunnel and comes to rest inside her home, breathing heavily. Pennyroyal approaches her wordlessly, and the two affectionately nuzzle one another.

"Mama, Mama!" shouts the previously inconsolable Cricket, burrowing her small head into her mother's body. Marigold and Shadow approach next, hesitantly. Mistletoe descends from his watch at the opening of the den, standing back a little from the loving reunion between Moon, Pennyroyal, and the kits.

Moon's normally serene face appears calm, but her eyes are full of apprehension. She has come home without any food. Hungry and exhausted, she lies down slowly against the wall of the den, allowing the kits to come and nurse from her.

"I know about the coyotes," she mutters to Pennyroyal plaintively. Her mate shifts his feet anxiously. When she remains quiet, he relays his own experience with Thorn and the conditions that must be met for the foxes to keep their territory.

"I see," she replies when he finishes. "I did not say anything to Ruby or Tomboy because I was trying to get home, but the mate of the one-eyed coyote you spoke to chased me away from the hunting field, and I have been hiding from her. Every time I would attempt to take another route to find food, she followed me and growled and snapped at me so that I couldn't hunt. Her name is Nettle—she told me as much when she was snapping at my hind legs. Finally, early morning, she broke away and left me, but I was too afraid to come out until daylight. Where there is one coyote, there are certainly more." Moon's face grows pensive as she speaks, the white stripe above her brows softly illuminated in the dim light of the den. "I do not know what we should do."

"I do not trust Thorn," imparts Pennyroyal with quiet conviction, "but we are not strong enough to withstand an attack. We must keep the knowledge of the coyote pack to ourselves for now until we can buy a little time and figure out what to do. Mistletoe," he says, turning to his oldest son, "you must go and find Francis immediately, before he breaks the news himself." Mistletoe nods his head once, and shoots out the den, quicker than lightning. Pennyroyal again addresses his family. "I will go out hunting and find us something to eat. Let's hope the coyotes got their fill of mischief and have retired for the day. I won't stray far." And like a flash, Pennyroyal follows Mistletoe out of the den.

"Mama, what's a coyote?" asks Cricket sleepily after her brother and father have left.

"A coyote is a very cunning creature, my dear, and they generally also have bad tempers. They can be dangerous, and we do not share territories with them."

"But I thought foxes were the cleverest of all the animals," chimes in Marigold, who is trying to appear as knowledgeable as Moon.

"We are, my dear, but coyotes are more dangerous than foxes and should be avoided."

"Ah," murmurs Marigold knowingly, although a question still lingers around her face, so like her mother's.

"Hush now; we're safe. Let's sleep," coos Moon to her kits with just a hint of a quiver in her voice. The four foxes snuggle together and fall asleep.

Chapter 4
THE SEARCH TO FIND FRANCIS

It is daylight, and the world seems to shimmer to Mistletoe's eyes. He must find Francis, the raven, and instruct him not to tell Farmer Reynolds's animals about the coyotes until the foxes can come up with a plan. Normally, Francis would be lining up with Mrs. Reynolds's chickens for breakfast about now. Mistletoe sprints as fast as he can, scouring the sky and trees for the black image of the raven. He must get to Francis before Francis gossips with the chickens. If he tells the chickens, they will surely tell Ruby, who will then inform Tomboy of the coyotes, and the treaty the foxes have with the dog may be in jeopardy. After searching the field and the tree line of the forest, Mistletoe makes his way to the farmhouse and the chicken yard. Because of the treaty, he has never been so close to the house by himself. When he was still a kit last year, Pennyroyal had shown him the layout of the farmhouse and its property and related to him the history of the foxes' treaty with the cat and dog. But they had remained on the fence line separating the house proper from the dove hunting meadow, which leads out to the forest and the den. Today, Mistletoe slips under the wooden fence and trots toward the house. The grass is mowed here, and in the sunshine, his red body stands out like a sore thumb. He keeps low to the ground to try and camouflage himself as much as possible.

The chicken yard is on the northwest side of the house to the left of the old red barn where Farmer Reynolds keeps his farming equipment. The cows have a smaller stable adjacent to the pasture behind the house where they feed. Mistletoe slinks up the driveway, his hair bristling as he contemplates the big windows on the front of the farmhouse. The farmer's old rusty blue pickup is not in the driveway, which means that both he and Tomboy aren't home, for the dog goes everywhere the farmer does.

Mrs. Reynolds keeps well-tended bushes of her prize-winning roses all around the house, and Mistletoe uses these for cover. The roses' thorns scratch at his back and legs, but Mistletoe ignores them, breathing heavily, and weaves his way under the bushes to the back of the house. He moves slowly to avoid the thorns and to elude detection. As he makes his way to the back of Farmer Reynolds's homestead, the chicken yard comes into view. The chickens are out and feeding on the corn Mrs. Reynolds has strewn out for them. Mistletoe pauses for a moment, looking over the yard for Francis. Inching closer, he sees the hens pecking at the feed and each other, but no sign of the raven. Or of Mrs. Reynolds, who is inside the white clapboard house, clucking away on the telephone.

He doesn't dare come any closer. The chickens would likely fly into a terror if they saw a fox so near their coop, and that would be just as bad as Francis showing up and spilling the news about the coyotes. After waiting a moment more to survey the scene, Mistletoe turns around underneath the protective cover of the rose bushes, intending to circle back to the front of the house and back to the fence line. Francis sometimes spends time chatting with the crows in the cornfield that lies beyond the cow pasture at the northernmost portion of Farmer Reynolds's property. The fox knows he can access the cornfield through the woods and avoid crossing over the cow pasture altogether.

As Mistletoe stoops beneath a bevy of red roses, the front door opens and closes, and Ruby the calico cat jumps off the front porch. Unaware of the fox hiding under the bushes, Ruby stretches her body luxuriously in a patch of sunlight. Mistletoe freezes, a large thorn pressing into the side of his head. Ruby would surely alert Tomboy of the fox's presence if she knew he were there, but she seems to be blissfully ignorant of his presence. Mistletoe is on the south-western corner of the house, and an easternly breeze is blowing, effectively blocking his scent. When Ruby is finally finished stretching, her calico fur glistening in the sun's rays, she advances slowly around the porch to the other side of the house, away from Mistletoe's hiding place. Relieved, he untangles himself from the roses, and moves full speed in the direction of the fence line and the dove hunting meadow beyond.

He doesn't stop running until he makes it to the tree line of the forest, then slows to a trot as he enters the woods. The sun has warmed away the shadows on the forest floor, and everything is emerald green in the dappled light dancing through the swaying leaves. As he weaves his way through the underbrush, he passes the fallen tree of the fox den. He pauses momentarily to contemplate whether he should check in on Moon and the kits, but instead continues his search for Francis. Mistletoe feels the faintest sense of panic since he hasn't found the bird yet. He trusts his father, but Pennyroyal had no plan beyond stalling to tell Ruby and Tomboy about the coyotes. Mistletoe has never met a coyote before, but he knows from his mother's stories that they aren't to be trusted. And this Thorn sounds like an evil character. Where could Francis be?

Across the path Mistletoe is following, a large rabbit hops out. The fox stops, his stomach grumbling. Distracted, he watches the rabbit bounce along slowly, its nose quivering. Suddenly, the hare's ears twitch, his eyes widen, and, catching the scent of the hunter, he bounds off, abruptly concealing himself in bushes nearby. Mistletoe begins the chase, utterly forgetting his mission to find the raven and the danger of the coyotes. The rabbit leaps away from Mistletoe's clambering jaws, sprinting eastward into the woods. The fox and the rabbit rush along in this manner for several minutes. Mistletoe can think of nothing other than how delicious the prey will taste. The rabbit, for his part, can think of nothing other than saving his furry hide. Leaping with his great hind legs up a small hill, he bounds over the edge of an embankment, tumbling down into the stream of Big Creek. Mistletoe tumbles after, scrabbling at the side of the embankment to keep from falling in the water. The hare swims with effort to the other side of the creek, his eyes still wild with fear. Climbing up the opposite embankment to where Mistletoe stands, breath heaving, the rabbit takes one look back at his predator, then shoots off into the trees.

There, on the other side of the creek, just above where the rabbit has escaped, stands the stag that appeared to Mistletoe and Shadow the night they encountered the strange tree deep in the forest. He is a ten-point buck, his antlers massive above his powerful body. He regards Mistletoe with a grave look. The fox, forgetting his appetite, stares back at the mysterious animal.

"My name is Ahwi." The stag's baritone voice is resonant over the soft bubbling of the creek below. There is a long pause, and in the silence, the two animals seem to communicate to one another without language. Mistletoe senses that he must trust Ahwi, although the stag's presence and form are as imposing as a bear's.

"My name is Mistletoe," declares the fox, finally returning the buck's greeting. Ahwi doesn't move; however, his eyes acknowledge what the fox has said.

"Mistletoe," the stag pronounces after another lengthy pause. "I know what you must do to defeat the coyotes." At the mention of the coyotes, Mistletoe remembers his quest to find the bird and frantically remembers how much time he has wasted. He tries to turn to leave, but finds himself rooted to the spot, transfixed by Ahwi's deep gaze. "You must meet me here tonight, and I will show you what to do."

Mistletoe's jaw drops slightly. If the stag Ahwi knows about their dilemma with the coyotes, then who else knows?

As if reading the Fox's mind, Ahwi then says, "Go find the raven. He is in the cornfield, as you suspected. Hurry." And with a flourish of his majestic head, the buck strides away from the embankment, disappearing into the trees.

Without delay, Mistletoe scrabbles up the side of the embankment over the creek, speeding back the way he came. When he regains the path that he was on before he spied the rabbit, he picks up his speed even more, rushing through the verdant foliage of the forest on his way to Farmer Reynolds's cornfield.

With the crops finally in sight past the thick tree line, Mistletoe sees Francis sitting on the scarecrow in the middle of the field, his black body punctuating the cloudless blue sky. The raven is alone, but the scarecrow is a gathering ground for birds of every nature. Mistletoe quickens his pace, flying up the rows of corn to the straw-stuffed puppet wearing Farmer Reynolds's old flannel shirt and work jeans.

"Hello there, Mistletoe!" shouts Francis loudly as the fox approaches. "It's a rootin'-tootin' fine morning, isn't it?"

Mistletoe slows his pace. Francis is in one of his moods where the world is full of poetry and song. He may even try to sing, God forbid. Clearly, the presence of the coyotes is not as big a concern for the bird as it was last night. Mistletoe sighs. Trying to impress upon the theatrical raven the seriousness of their situation may be more difficult than the fox had bargained for.

"*But when the fox hath once got in his nose, he'll soon find means to make the body follow,*" squawks Francis, quoting some line of poetry he has heard in his travels.

"Francis," begins Mistletoe timidly. "Francis, I need to talk to you about the coyotes you saw last night."

"*A fox never found a better messenger than himself.*" Francis chortles on with his verse and proverbs, oblivious to the plaintive tone in the fox's voice. Mistletoe sighs again. This could take all day, and Mistletoe doesn't have all day. Fatigued with hunger and lack of sleep, he eyes the bird with annoyance. Francis prattles on with his rhymes, pecking the scarecrow's face at odd intervals, as though he were tapping out a complicated meter on the blank staring eyes.

"Francis!" shouts Mistletoe, losing his patience. The raven shudders once, then again, then alights from the scarecrow's head and flies down to eye level with the perturbed fox.

"What you need is a good hot meal, Mistletoe!" shouts the raven back at the fox. Then, with a swiftness that manages to impress the fox, Francis buries his beak in the dirt between the rows of corn and comes back up with a juicy worm. He tosses the writhing worm to Mistletoe, who gobbles it down before he can think twice.

"Thank you, Francis. I was starving," Mistletoe grunts, licking his chops. Francis contemplates him with a solemn air, his head cocked to one side so he can get a better look at his visitor.

"You wanted to talk about the coyotes?" Francis prompts.

"Yes. You know we have a truce with Tomboy and Ruby that as long as we do not poach Farmer Reynolds's chickens, they will leave us alone. The coyotes have promised if we do not interfere with their business, then they will allow us to share the hunting territory. We know they mean to go after the chickens. Father—Pennyroyal—doesn't want to alert Ruby or Tomboy about the coyotes until we can come up with a plan." Mistletoe grimaces at this last statement, feeling the inadequacy of his position. Despite his meeting with Ahwi the stag, who promises to tell him how to defeat the coyotes, Mistletoe knows that the foxes are at the mercy of the new predators.

"Ah, yes. The truce. Ruby and Tomboy, Tomboy and Ruby. Cat and dog, dog and cat. Chickens. Oh yes, the chickens! I haven't seen them yet today! Whatever will they think when I tell them I saw a fox in broad daylight under the scarecrow!" And Francis prattles on again and hops from one black taloned foot to the other in front of the bewildered fox.

"You cannot tell the chickens, or Ruby, or Tomboy, or anyone else about the coyotes!" Mistletoe shouts to get the bird's attention. Francis stops hopping momentarily and contemplates what the fox has said. Abruptly, he takes wing, flying skyward so quickly that Mistletoe becomes dizzy watching his spiraling climb.

"Your secret is safe with me!" squawks the raven over his shoulder before his black form crests the first trees of the forest and recedes from view.

Pennyroyal watches his elder son scamper across the meadow away from the farmhouse and into the woods. He has been hunting nearly all morning and is about to go back to the den with a slew of mice and some acorns. The mouse problem has been under control for years, but these mice feel more comfortable under the protective light of day than at night, at the mercy of nocturnal predators like himself. He trusts that Mistletoe will find Francis the raven and stop the news of the coyotes from spreading to the farm animals. Back when Ruby and Tomboy first approached the foxes for help hunting the mice, Pennyroyal and Moon had just made their den beneath the fallen tree.

Ruby the cat had come up with the idea of asking the foxes for help. She was an experienced mouser herself and knew when she was in over her head. Tomboy had been more reluctant. The Labrador retriever was old back then and set in her ways. She had never approached a fox for help, or any other wild animal for that matter. Her job was to protect the farmer's property, including the chickens whose eggs made a nice meal for the dog when she had been especially good.

But Ruby and Tomboy were old friends, and Tomboy trusted that Ruby was being truthful when she said she could no longer keep up with the mice. Tomboy herself had no desire to spend her time chasing down rodents, and so she agreed with Ruby that something must be done and that something was to go to the new foxes that had just moved into the neighborhood.

The cat and dog used Francis to convey the message that the animals should meet by the fence line. So, the bird was there from the beginning too. Francis beat his wings silently over the meadow to the young fox and his vixen, and in a stately manner, orated that the farmer's dog and cat were proposing a treaty, and the pets requested their presence to determine the details. And lest the foxes think it was a trap, Ruby would come alone, for the pair of foxes could surely overpower a cat.

And so, Pennyroyal, Moon, and Ruby had met at the fence line between Farmer Reynolds's yard and the dove hunting meadow. Ruby explained that the mice were overtaking the yard, barn, and were even encroaching on the house. She said that they wanted the foxes to come past the fence each night, into the yard and the barn, and catch the mice. Ruby could manage the house by herself, but the rest was simply beyond her. As a show of good faith, Tomboy had promised her nightly feast of eggs to the foxes, and she herself would remain on the porch while Pennyroyal and Moon hunted. They were not to go near the chicken coop or the house. Ruby said that if they could uphold their end of the bargain, Tomboy would never knowingly put the foxes in danger and would lead Farmer Reynolds away from the den when he went out hunting.

The foxes had agreed, and later that night, feasted on mice and the eggs Mrs. Reynolds put in Tomboy's dish. They never approached the house and ignored the chickens, satisfied to remain bound by the treaty. It had taken a week for the foxes to bring the mouse problem under control, and because the farmer and his wife never suspected their animals of bargaining with wildlife, Ruby was treated to the upmost pampering and excess of affection any person could lavish upon a cat.

After the mouse hunting week had ended, Pennyroyal and Moon again met Ruby, this time accompanied by Tomboy, at the fence line.

"Thank you," Tomboy had said solemnly, her old eyes looking over the foxes with a measure of gratitude and suspicion.

"Yes, thank you," purred Ruby, her green eyes sleepy with unearned contentment.

As a thank you, the animals determined they would always share news that may concern each other, and the old black dog would continue to protect the den for as long as she was able, provided the foxes never cross the fence line again. Pennyroyal and Moon, being of good character, believed themselves to be the guardians of an important agreement and impressed upon the cat and dog the seriousness of their vow. Reassured, the animals parted ways, and over the years, proved themselves loyal to the treaty.

Pennyroyal considers all of this as he trots back to the den. Up until now, the treaty protected the foxes as they made their home and raised their kits on Farmer Reynolds's property. Now, with the appearance of the coyotes, that same treaty could put Pennyroyal and his family in jeopardy. He must decide which danger is the greater threat. If he tells Tomboy and Ruby about the coyotes, Thorn and his gang will surely terrorize the foxes until they either leave their den or are killed. However, if he keeps the matter to himself, the farm animals will become aware of the coyotes eventually. Tomboy would surely take such an event to mean that the treaty had been broken and would hunt the foxes herself. Pennyroyal sighs heavily, feeling the burden of a decision weighing down on him.

But what if there is another way? The red fox pauses outside the den, an idea occurring to him. Yes, it was possible, but he was unsure where she was resting this time of year. He continued to think, dropping the mice and nuts at the mouth of the den—Moon would find them—and suddenly, like a red streak, he races in the direction of Maw Maw and Paw Paw, the gopher tortoises.

Chapter 5

THORN

Thorn was born in the oldest town in Texas in a storm grate with four other pups. The city of Nacogdoches had long been home to coyotes, as increased urbanization across the Southeast displaced thousands of animals from their natural habitat, including bobcats and foxes. Coyotes are intelligent animals, however, and very adaptable. When the freight train from Houston rolled into town, the whistle would incite a dozen coyotes into a chorus of vocalizations that sounded like a hundred wild dogs. There were plenty of old, abandoned buildings for Thorn and his brothers and sisters to find shelter, and for the young pup, the whole world was built of concrete and steel.

For their part, Thorn's parents had lived on the

outskirts of the Deep East Texas town their whole lives, getting ever closer to the city limits as the population increased. Thorn's litter was their second, and as their family grew, so did their need for food. They became expert garbage pickers. The animals always thought it incredible what humans threw in the trash. They also feasted on the abundance of mice and rats that seemed bred to live in a town and the occasional rabbit.

One evening in early fall, as Thorn was out hunting with his mother and siblings, they entered a suburban area of the city. Hunting in a city was always a challenge, and new territories were needed as more and more wildlife crept into town. The driveways of this area were long and stretched in dark rows up to the cheerfully lit houses, and at the end of each one sat a green city garbage can. Thorn and his siblings salivated as the smell of discarded food wafted over the night air. They began by knocking over one of the cans, its contents spilling out over the driveway. One of the bags tore open as it rolled over the concrete, revealing a slew of chicken bones from a fast-food restaurant. The coyote pups began devouring the bones as their mother knocked over another can with her forepaws.

The animals were so intent upon their supper they did not notice the young boy in the coon skin hat who had crept up on them through the darkness of the yard. In his hands rested a large metal BB gun. As he walked closer, his every footstep chosen with care so as not to disturb his prey, he lifted the gun to his shoulder, closing one eye to take better aim at the raiders. The streetlight overhead illuminated the coyotes, but he stood in the shadows, waiting for his shot.

And it came. Pulling the trigger, the projectile from the gun hit Thorn's mother in the hindquarters, her face immersed in an old can of tuna. Yelping, she scrambled backward, her right hind leg wounded and limping. The pups, alarmed at the sudden commotion, howled for their mother and scurried after her. All of them except Thorn. He turned in the direction of the gunfire and, sighting the boy, began approaching him, his head lowered and snarling. Surprised, the boy hoisted up his gun a second time and took aim at Thorn's head. The second shot landed with explosive force, tearing into the coyote's flesh and blinding one dark eye. Barking in pain, Thorn fled, trailing blood down the black driveway. The boy ran inside the house, shouting to his father that he shot not one but two coyotes.

Thorn's family had managed to escape and returned to the abandoned building near the old train museum that served as their den. Thorn convalesced there until his wound healed, a scarred over hole where the eye had been—a constant reminder of his tangle with a human. It was not to be his last. The city of Nacogdoches had started an initiative to clean up the streets from the wildlife that was encroaching on the town and its residents. The coyotes were targeted as a public nuisance, and animal control officials were permitted to trap and exterminate them at will. Thorn's mother was permanently injured from the BB gun, and she ran with a limp. One day, as she was scavenging garbage near the high school, she found herself caught in a trap. Thorn never saw her again. His brothers and sisters likewise disappeared. Full of animosity toward humans, the young coyote fled Nacogdoches and its inhabitants in search of new territory.

He followed the highway east out of town, entering the great piney woods between the Texas and Louisiana state line. For a long time, he stayed close to the great paved roadway that cut like a river between the towering trees on either side. There was plenty of garbage to eat that the humans threw out of their automobiles, and other scavengers, like raccoons or possums, tended to stay away from the lone coyote making his way through the great forest.

He had already walked many miles when, one evening, he noticed a black form moving between the trees in time with his own pace. When he turned to get a better look, it had disappeared. Thorn paused his wandering, looking all around him. He was certain that he had seen something, but nothing was there. Shaking his head with confusion, he continued his journey.

A few hours later, as the mist lay over the road and trees, with only the beam of occasional headlights cutting through, Thorn noticed the black form again, only this time, it was closer and following behind him. He could only make out the faintest line of a silhouette moving slowly and deliberately, and a luminous, predatory eye shine in the darkness. Quickening, Thorn darted over the road, directly in front of a semi-truck that blared its horn at the coyote as he crossed to the other side of the highway to escape whatever was stalking him. He watched the road patiently but didn't see any animals crossing over behind him. Satisfied whoever was no longer following, he walked in the same direction as before.

The hour was very late, and Thorn was hungry. Tired of eating the waste thrown on the side of the road, he veered off into the woods surrounding the highway like a great black blanket. As he traveled deeper between the trees, his hunter's spirit came alive. He could smell a rabbit nearby and put his nose to the soft dirt of the forest floor to better pick out its scent. Detecting his prey hiding behind a nearby bush, the coyote crept softly on silent paws to just behind the foliage concealing the rabbit. He waited for a breath, and then leapt into the bush to flush the terrified animal from her hiding place. She was a hair too late in leaping with her great hind legs away from her death, and Thorn's powerful jaws clamped down on her throat mercilessly. Satisfied that she was dead, the coyote carried the carcass a little ways further into the obscurity of the woods, then sat down and feasted on his kill.

After he had finished, Thorn felt the energy of the rabbit enter his blood. Alert, he trotted through the trees, surveying his territory. He spotted a doe in the mist, her brown hide glistening with dewdrops. He became perfectly still as he gazed at the deer, who was unaware of his presence, grazing silently in the night. The rabbit slaked his hunger, but Thorn's senses vibrated with anticipation. This was what he was born to do, and he felt it in every cell of his body. He lowered his head ever so slightly and prepared to give chase. The doe had raised her head, sensing something in the trees, but the coyote blended into the dark landscape, and she did not see him. Thorn's shoulder muscles twitched, and like a dagger, he flew through the air at the deer.

Just as Thorn leapt into motion, a deafening roar shook the forest, and a Southern black puma descended from the tree above Thorn like an invisible flash, pouncing on the unsuspecting coyote and pinning him to the ground beneath its muscular body. Black pumas are thought by "scientific types" to not exist, but there have been sightings of the mysterious large cats since time immemorial in the Southeast. This one didn't care what humans believed or didn't believe about it. It had been stalking Thorn since the morning without the coyote's knowledge and was now grinding its razor claws into his back, swishing its great dark tail back and forth through the air like a whip.

"Who are you?" Thorn grunted, trying to lift his body but unable to move. The puma dug its claws deeper into his fur, cutting into his flesh.

"I am Death," said the huge black cat, and lifting Thorn up with its claws, threw him against a nearby tree. Thorn hit the tree with a thud and collapsed on the ground. The puma leapt on him again, batting him from one fierce paw to the other. Thorn's head rattled with the force of the blows. His one eye perceived the animal's form in the darkness—a black monster full of murderous intent. With another powerful slap, Thorn skidded across the ground, his motion halted by the trunk of another tree.

The puma waited, sitting back on its haunches, preparing to strike again. With a terrible roar, it launched itself at the coyote. Just before its claws could again make purchase in Thorn's flesh, he rolled away as fast as he could push himself. The great cat landed with tremendous force on empty ground, scrabbling into the undergrowth. Thorn regained his feet and prepared to fight. The puma's luminous eyes narrowed in the velvet shadow of its face, a low growl of anger emanating from its mouth. They stared at each other for a long moment, each assessing the other with predatory calculation. Then Thorn broke the silence with a great howl and leapt at the puma just as it jumped toward the coyote in attack.

Despite his wounds, Thorn was faster than the cat. He bit down as hard as he could on its foreleg, scraping its face with his claws. The puma hissed and scrambled away; its ears laid back on its curved head. Just as quickly, it countered and swiped Thorn across the muzzle, leaving a trail of scratches. Thorn ducked his head to protect his throat and leapt at the puma again. Knocking it off balance, he lunged into the great black beast, clamping his jaws down on the back of its neck. The cat roared with pain and discontent, shaking its body to try and loosen the coyote's grip. But Thorn didn't let go. He plunged his sharp teeth deeper into the folds of flesh, black fur choking the back of his throat, and slammed the cat down on the ground.

The foliage and trees began to rustle with small animals gathering to watch the fight. Thorn and the puma battled through the night until their blood soaked the forest floor. As dawn approached, the black puma managed to pull loose from the coyote's ferocious jaws and fled into the glowing mist hovering between the trees. Thorn watched the animal that had almost killed him flee, and then he collapsed on the ground where he stood and slept.

When Thorn woke, sunlight was streaming in through the trees. It was mid-March, but the temperature was mild. Rising to his feet, he felt every scratch and wound the puma had inflicted upon him. Still exhausted, the coyote slowly plodded through the forest.

Coming to a clear pool between the massive pines, Thorn padded to the edge of the bank, and slumping down, contemplated his reflection in the still water. He was not handsome—his appearance was somewhat ghoulish on account of the missing eye and the cuts from the puma's claws—but he was intelligent, and, after the fight with the puma, he knew he was strong. Thorn took all this in, and bending his head to the water, began to drink.

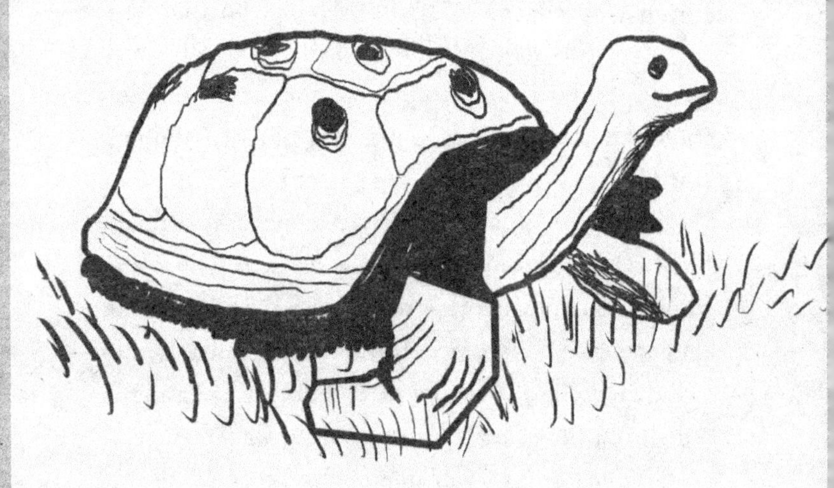

Chapter 6

A PLAN IS BORN

Maw Maw and Paw Paw are the oldest animals in Big Creek, with a collective lifespan of 160 years. Their shells are dark green mottled with gray, and their eyes are full of years and wisdom. All the animals know them and pay them respect, and they readily provide any useful information to whomever may need it, for the tortoises know everything that goes on in the community, with the humans and animals alike. Mistletoe has been hanging around a lot lately, listening to stories about what Big Creek was like one hundred years ago. He especially likes the stories of the sharecropper and his family, although their tale is somewhat tragic—the sharecropper's wife couldn't hold a child in her belly, and their babies are buried in the forest where they lived, like a sad memory. A good Southern fox, Mistletoe cherishes the history of his territory. Maw Maw and Paw Paw are happy to oblige; they're good-natured beasts and care for the creatures of Big Creek.

Today, the ancient tortoises are in a field near their burrow, munching grass in the hot Alabama June heat. In the distance, they can see a red image streaking toward them like a fireball. At first, they think it is Mistletoe coming by for another social visit, but as the blazing shape grows closer, they recognize him as Pennyroyal, leader of the foxes.

"Pennyroyal. Hello," greets Paw Paw, raising his scaly head to meet the fox's eye. The tortoise can tell at once that Pennyroyal has come on an urgent mission. Paw Paw swallows the last bite of grass in his mouth and nods his head at the red fox, giving him permission to speak.

"I'm sorry to come this way, but it is an emergency. Coyotes are in Big Creek, and they have threatened my family if I don't cooperate with them. The treaty with Ruby and Tomboy is in peril, and the coyotes mean to harm Farmer Reynolds and his chickens. I need your help."

"How can we help you, Pennyroyal?" Maw Maw asks the fox, her old eyes looking kindly into his serious face.

"I have a plan, I think, but I need to know where Ursa is sleeping this time of year." Pennyroyal regards the tortoises soberly as they exchange a look with each other. Maw Maw turns her wizened face to her mate, nodding once.

Paw Paw states, "She has made her den in a hollowed-out tree near the duck pond. She will be highly active this time of year, Pennyroyal, so I advise you to be cautious." The old reptile returns the fox's stare, this time with gravity. Pennyroyal takes a step back from the pair and bows his head low before them in thanks before darting off from whence he came.

The hot sun beats down on him as he makes his way swiftly back to the den. Tonight, he will meet with Thorn and his coyotes and discuss a new treaty with them. If it works, the invaders will be ousted by the next night. Pennyroyal scans the tree line for Mistletoe. If the young fox has been successful, his father will have time to tell Moon and the others his plan, and the coyotes will no longer be a threat. As the sticky heat of a wet Alabama afternoon fills Pennyroyal's panting mouth, he coughs once and enters the den, primed with the force of his idea.

The den is cooler within than outside, but not enough for the kits to sleep. Shadow, Marigold, and Cricket turn to look at their father as he darts down the tunnel. Moon has found the dead mice as Pennyroyal had predicted, and after feeding the kits and herself, curled up against the den wall to try and find some rest. Pennyroyal goes to her, nuzzling her head with his nose. She awakens, and shaking the sleep from her eyes, rises to her feet.

"Pennyroyal, what is it? Are the coyotes back?" Moon looks around her, still slightly disoriented from her sleep. The kits huddle together, sensing the fear in their mother.

"No, but I have a plan to get rid of them. Has Mistletoe returned?" Pennyroyal glances around the den anxiously, searching for his older son. Moon raises a questioning brow at her mate and shakes her head no.

"Tell me your plan," she says, going over to the kits and giving each a comforting lick on the muzzle. Cricket breaks away from her siblings and sidles up to Moon, burying her head into her mother's furry hide.

"Thorn said we will meet again tonight to discuss terms of a new treaty with the coyotes. I'm going to take him to the duck pond to hunt for eggs. Ursa is sleeping there, and she will drive Thorn and his pack away." Pennyroyal locks eyes with Moon, an idea passing between them.

"Ursa?" Moon exclaims, her brows arching higher with surprise. "She's dangerous, Pennyroyal. She could kill you—"

"I know, my darling, but she is our only hope." The fox stares steadily at his mate, and her eyes soften with love for him. Pennyroyal is the rock upon which their family is built. Foolish as his plan may seem, she believes him when he says there is no other way.

Moon breathes in deeply and says, "I will do whatever you need me to do." Her mate gives her a grim smile, his own eyes radiating the love between them.

"I need to find Mistletoe. You and he will have to help me maintain the other coyotes until we find Ursa."

"I want to help too, Father! Let me come with you!" Shadow steps toward Pennyroyal, his tail wagging with anticipation, ready to fight.

"No, son. I need you to stay here and protect your sisters." Pennyroyal looks kindly at his son, but his voice is stern. Shadow lowers his eyes quickly to conceal his hurt.

Marigold looks from her brother to her father, then steps up, saying authoritatively, "I'll make sure we're safe, Father, and that no one leaves the den."

"Thank you, Marigold. That's enough," chimes Moon softly from the corner where she has begun nursing Cricket. Marigold buttons her lip but gazes meaningfully at her father. Pennyroyal ignores her and turns back to Moon.

"I have to go find Mistletoe. Meet me at the scarecrow just after dusk, Moon. I will tell you the rest of the plan there."

"Are we going to find Thorn? How will we know where he is?" Moon's face has become apprehensive as Pennyroyal starts to ascend the tunnel out of the den.

He turns his head to look at her, and before darting out of the den, says, "He will find us."

Mistletoe walks away from the scarecrow in the direction that Francis went. Now that he has safely prevented the bird from telling the farm about the coyotes, he mulls over everything that has happened since the morning. Most importantly, he thinks about Ahwi, the stag, and how he must meet him tonight to discover how to defeat the coyotes.

As he enters the cool shade of the forest, his thoughts drift to food. The worm that Francis foraged up for him has barely satiated his appetite, and he can feel his stomach grumble for a meal. He must find Pennyroyal and tell him about the stag's appearance, but for now the scent of blueberries in the forest preoccupies him. Finding a bush full of them, Mistletoe stops and eats his fill of the sweet fruit.

As Mistletoe buries his head further in the bush,

picking off the berries with his tongue, Pennyroyal approaches from behind. The younger fox pulls his head back abruptly from his foraging, swallowing the last of the blueberries noisily. For a moment, father and son simply regard one another, and then Pennyroyal breaks the silence and addresses his son.

"Did you find Francis?" The older fox asks patiently.

"Yes, and he promised not to speak of the coyotes. Father—" but Pennyroyal cuts off Mistletoe.

"That's good, Mistletoe, that's good. I want you to meet me tonight at the scarecrow with your mother. I have a plan to drive the coyotes away from here, but I will need your help."

"But Father, today in the forest—"

"Not now, Mistletoe. This is urgent. We can discuss whatever it is later. For now, I need you to promise you will meet me at the scarecrow."

Mistletoe looks his father in the eye and sighs. When Pennyroyal takes it into his head to do something, there is no dissuading him. Mistletoe would like to tell him about Ahwi and how the stag said that he would show him how to defeat the coyotes, but he can't get a word in edgewise to tell Pennyroyal. Besides, Pennyroyal has settled on a plan, and nothing will stop his determination to follow it through, even the appearance of a mysterious stag.

"Yes, Father. I will meet you tonight at the scarecrow." Mistletoe notices with subdued affection the pleased look Pennyroyal takes. Nodding once to his son, the older fox leaps away into the bushes, his red tail a blaze against the blueberries. Mistletoe listens to the sound of his father's steps retreating into the forest back to the den, then mumbles to himself, "I will meet you there, Father. But I won't stay."

That night, after dusk, Moon rises within the den and performs a luxurious stretch from her toes to her tail. The eyes of her kits are like pools of light in the dark, and Moon regards them each with tenderness. They listen to their mother attentively as she instructs them to stay in the den and not leave. She is not as authoritative as Pennyroyal, but tonight, she is not only their mother but a warrior. Their father fetched more mice and berries for the kits to hold them over until morning, then left the den and had not returned. Moon is going to meet him now.

As Moon ascends the mouth of the tunnel and vanishes from sight, Shadow rises in the darkness and starts to leave the den. Suddenly, Marigold stands before him, the white stripe on her forehead glowing like a star.

"Shadow, no way. Mama told us to stay in the den." but Shadow just brushes past her. There is something so cool in his demeanor that Marigold simply stands gaping after him as he trots to the opening beneath the fallen tree. Looking back once at his sisters, he darts off toward the scarecrow and his parents.

The evening is as oppressively hot as the day was, and Shadow shakes the heat from his fur before continuing in the direction his mother went. He can see her form disappearing into the woods traveling northeast, and keeping a safe distance, follows her. He has never gone into the forest unaccompanied, and the thrill of his independence tingles through his nerve endings. The sun has crossed the threshold of the western horizon, and the burgeoning night pulsates with magic. Shadow can feel every sound and scent vibrating within him, full of possibility. He follows his mother, careful not to make her aware of his presence trailing behind. She stays close to the tree line, trotting purposefully, pausing every now and again to assess her surroundings.

After a while, Moon comes out from the cover of the woods into the open cornfield. Shadow stops inside the forest, watching her as she travels up the neat green rows of corn toward the old scarecrow in the middle of the field. The world has succumbed completely to darkness, and Moon appears almost gray in the starlight. Another fox, larger than herself, is waiting for her there. Taking a deep breath, the young fox exits the tree line and begins weaving up the rows of corn behind his mother, still without her knowledge.

Just as Shadow loses sight of Moon in the cornfield, Mistletoe rushes up on him from behind.

"Hey, kid," Shadow's older brother says, slowing his pace. "Whatcha doin' out here on this fine evening?" Mistletoe's eyes twinkle as he circles around Shadow, who is startled and has stopped moving altogether.

"Mistletoe! I, I, I'm out looking for—" Shadow stammers, unable to come up with an excuse. Mistletoe shakes his head in mock disapproval, the hint of a smile in his eyes. Shadow stops talking, shifting from one paw to the other as he looks up at his brother from lowered eyes.

"Look, little brother, you know you shouldn't be creeping around by yourself; there are coyotes about. Since I found you sneaking out and going where you don't belong, your only choice," and Mistletoe lowers himself down so that he is at eye level with Shadow, who is staring at his paws, "your only choice is to stick with me."

Shadow blinks a couple times, then looks up at Mistletoe, smiling slightly.

"Hang back," the older fox tells his little brother. "I'm going to go talk to Pennyroyal and see what he wants. You stay out of sight. There's someplace else I have to be tonight, and maybe, if you're good," and here Mistletoe looks at Shadow levelly, "you can come with me."

"All right, Mistletoe!" Shadow yips, and then lowering his voice, whispers, "I mean, I'll do whatever you say."

"Excellent," says Shadow's older brother, then turning, trots off in the direction of the scarecrow.

When he arrives, Pennyroyal and Moon are deep in conversation. Pennyroyal, who was sitting, stands to greet his son, then sits back down and resumes talking.

"As I was telling your mother, after I left the den, I went to the duck pond. I found Ursa's lair. She's been living in a tree there on the edge of the water. Tonight, when Thorn and his gang approach us, we will lead them to the pond in search of duck eggs as a show of good faith. There, we will rouse Ursa, and she will drive out the coyotes."

Pennyroyal continues speaking softly, laying out his plan of trickery. His voice drifts softly over the green stalks of corn, slipping into the night on a breath. Then, without warning, the coyotes appear in the darkness.

MARIE LEVEAU

Chapter 7

NETTLE

Thorn continued following the highway east until he came to Alexandria, and then began following a different road south. He had no idea where he was going, but he felt that he would know when he got there. News of his defeat of the black puma had spread throughout the forest in Louisiana, and he was feared by everything. Catching prey was difficult because all the animals were on high alert, but he managed to avoid starving through his cunning. He became an expert in lying in wait for an unsuspecting rabbit or squirrel, and twice robbed a doe of her fawn. He never felt guilt for hunting; he was just trying to survive.

As he traveled deeper south, the terrain began to change to wet marshes and swampy bayous. Thorn picked his way through the mud, careful not to stir up snakes or alligators as he made his way. He began to hunt ducks and feast on their eggs, as the birds were very plentiful in that region. Night after night, day after day, Thorn wandered, never losing the road, until he found himself on a lonely stretch of beach facing the blue-green water of the Gulf of Mexico. It was beautiful to him. He sat for a long while, contemplating the water and the lovely waves rolling to shore. The tide was in, and Thorn felt a sense of peace wash over him, something he had never felt before. A long time passed before he began walking again, but when he did, he followed the coast and frequently stopped to admire the water before continuing his journey.

Thorn had begun walking east again, and the marshes were thick with mud. He had to walk further inland to avoid swimming, as the water reached in great swampy fingers up the boot-toe of Louisiana. Eventually, he came to a bayou town called Jean Lafitte. Instead of skirting the town as he had done others previously, he decided to venture into it and scavenge a quick meal. By this time, the coyote was an expert hunter, but the temptation of food easily obtained overcame him, leading him along a gravel road out to a boat dock that smelled of trash cans and fish.

To the right of the dock was a small building,

outside of which trash cans lined in a row overflowed their contents. Not seeing anyone, Thorn trotted toward the row of cans. The smell of saltwater and fish grew stronger as Thorn approached the dock. Keeping close to the building, he sniffed the first can, which smelled of fast food. The remains of a cheeseburger lay on the ground near it, and Thorn gobbled it up hungrily. In this late afternoon in May, the sun had not set yet. Alert for humans, the stealthy coyote scavenged the discarded food from the ground, unwilling to knock over the cans to avoid attracting attention.

As Thorn ate, he suddenly found himself nose to nose with a female coyote. She was thin—starving thin—and her fur was patchy and dull. Startled from her own meal, she looked at Thorn with a mixture of alarm and ferocity. Baring her teeth, she lowered her head, a low growl emanating from her narrow throat.

"Get out of here. This is my turf," she snarled. Thorn was so surprised to see another coyote that at first he didn't realize she was preparing to fight him. When he did come to his senses, he almost laughed at her. She was scrawny and looked weak enough to knock over with a playful pat. Still, Thorn backed off a few paces, reluctant to incite her to further fury. When he moved, her eyes bulged with fear, but she took a step closer, indicating she meant business.

"My name is Thorn. I've been traveling a long

time and just wanted something to eat. Look, I'm leaving. See? No harm intended." He backed off a little ways, and turning to go, looked back over his shoulder at the vicious little coyote behind him.

Just then, a human voice came from the building. The two coyotes froze, eyes locked. The female coyote let out a small whine and then disappeared. Thorn hesitated, then sneaked behind the building as the door opened and a man and a small dog exited.

"Come on now, Tinkerbell. We got shrimpin' to do." A swarthy man with dark stubble and half a cigar clamped between his yellow teeth emerged. At his feet danced a little mutt, presumably Tinkerbell, with a curly tail and red fur. The dog looked at the man expectantly as she hopped up and down, her eyes fixed on something in the man's calloused hands. The man regarded his small companion, smirking at the little animal's frenetic energy as he cupped whatever had captured the dog's attention. After a moment of teasing, the man opened his palm to reveal a sardine. He held it over Tinkerbell's nose, just out of reach, and laughed uproariously as the dog began leaping, trying to catch the little fish, over and over again. Finally, the man relented and tossed the fish to the mutt, who gobbled it up greedily.

As soon as Tinkerbell finished devouring the sardine, she began growling and barking at something hidden under a broken upside-down flat-bottomed boat leaning against the opposite side of the building from the trash cans.

"Watcha got there under the pirogue, Tinkerbell?" said the man in a thick Cajun accent. He strutted over to the dog, who was barking frantically. The man grunted as he stooped down to see what had the dog so worked up. There, underneath the boat, visible through its broken floorboard, was the female coyote. She watched the dog and the man with wide, angry eyes and growled menacingly as the man crouched closer to her hiding spot. He chewed his cigar thoughtfully, then stood up slowly.

Turning to the dog, he said, "Hold her tight, Tinkerbell. Be right back." And he disappeared inside the building. Tinkerbell continued barking and pacing back and forth in front of the broken boat, making an escape for the scrawny coyote impossible. She curled her lips back, baring a neat row of dagger sharp teeth. The dog increased her barking, the sound echoing off the water, which lay still and gray under a cloudy sky. The man reappeared in the doorway. In his hands he held a black revolver, and he paused a moment as he deposited brass-colored bullets into the circular chamber. After he loaded the gun, he walked around the back of the building to Tinkerbell and the boat.

"All right. Back off, Tink, back off!" the man

commanded the dog, and reluctantly, the mutt backed off a few paces, still barking. The man approached the boat with careful steps. Crouching down, he very slowly drew the gun up, pointing it through the hole at the terrified little coyote shivering under the boat. Squinting, he prepared to take aim. Tinkerbell restlessly barked in the background, but the man was as still as a statue, his dark eyes never leaving the trapped animal. The smoke from his cigar permeated the air. He breathed out a stream of smoke, his grip on the gun tightening, and as his finger squeezed the trigger—

Thorn exploded from behind the man, knocking him to the ground with a ferocious push from his forepaws. The revolver fired, but Thorn's attack had interrupted the man's aim, and the bullet missed its target, ricocheting off the building and landing in the dirt. The female coyote, seeing her attacker temporarily disabled, scrambled out of the hole in the boat and vanished behind the building. Tinkerbell, whose insistent barks had doubled at Thorn's appearance, raced after the female coyote as she made her escape. The man, knocked off his feet, regained his stance and turned his gun to Thorn. Thorn lunged at him, his jaws clamping down on the man's wrist, shaking the gun loose where it dropped harmlessly to the ground. The man yelped in surprise, the stinking cigar tumbling from his lips. He took his free hand

and began beating Thorn around the head to release his hand from the coyote's teeth, but Thorn held fast, ignoring the blows. The man dropped to his knees, his face stricken with alarm and pain. Finally, Thorn let go, leaving the man on the ground clutching his wounded arm to his chest and whimpering.

After releasing the man, the one-eyed coyote ran after the female behind the building. There, on the ground, lay Tinkerbell, dead. A few yards away, the little coyote crouched, her eyes wild. Her body quivered, and she didn't seem to see Thorn at first. He approached her slowly, careful not to make any sudden movements.

"Are you alone here?" Thorn questioned her. Startled by his voice, she blinked at the one-eyed coyote for a moment, stopped shivering, and regained her composure.

"You saved my life," she said, her voice gravelly with unuse. Thorn was about to speak further, but the man came stumbling around the corner of the building, his wrist bound in his shirt, the gun held in his other hand. When he saw the body of his little dog, the man let out a tremendous wail.

"Tink! Tink! Oh my god, you killed my dog! You'll pay for this!" The shirtless man raised the gun precariously, aiming at the coyotes. Thorn lowered his head and growled. The man's face was stricken.

He fired, hitting the ground in front of their feet and spraying gravel. Both coyotes leapt backward. The man raised the gun again, and Thorn leapt at him, knocking him on his back. As he fell, the gun fired again, missing Thorn by inches.

As he lay there, unconscious, a soft groan escaped from his lips. Thorn stood over the man, then turned back to the female coyote, his one good eye regarding her.

"What's your name?" Thorn asked the little female coyote.

"Nettle." She whispered her name, her eyes full of excitement and something deeper, like sorrow.

"Come with me, Nettle, and we shall be conquerors of the world." Thorn walked past her and continued back up the gravel road, away from the carnage of the man and his dog. Momentarily, Nettle joined him, walking by his side as though she had always been there.

The pair of coyotes began traveling north from Jean Lafitte. By August, they had made it to New Orleans, and Nettle was heavily pregnant. The weather was sweltering hot and humid, even at night, and the city was dense with people at all hours. Thorn and Nettle took to hunting rats and stray animals as they made their way through the concrete jungle. Before they gained their exit from the city, Nettle gave birth to two pups in an old cemetery during a terrible thunderstorm. The wind howled menacingly. It was midnight, and as Nettle labored to bring her offspring into the world, it seemed as though the very air was electrified with the spirits of the dead. When the two pups, a boy and a girl, were delivered, Nettle looked them over, licking each tenderly.

"His name is Ghost," she said, referring to the larger of the pups. "And her name is Voodoo."

The coyote family stayed in the cemetery for a month, making their den in one of the old, decrepit mausoleums. Thorn hunted at night for his family, stalking like a wraith through the city. He was so stealthy that humans never suspected his presence. When the pups were big enough, Thorn and Nettle urged them out of the crypt one night and began walking north. Ghost and Voodoo followed silently behind their parents. Born in a grave, they knew the world was cruel, and so said nothing because words were a waste.

Chapter 8

THE DUCK POND

Shadow watches as the coyotes approach the scarecrow slowly. He is crouching low to the ground, out of sight in the cornfield, but he can still make out the deadly eyeshine of his enemies. Mistletoe stands alongside Pennyroyal and Moon. He occasionally checks for Shadow, without attracting attention to him. Shadow has never seen a coyote before, and as they approach, a shiver slips down his spine.

The leader of the gang, a large, one-eyed coyote, breaks off from his pack and trots toward the three foxes. The three other coyotes stop and sit down in the cornrows. Shadow can barely see them between the large green leaves of the cornstalks, but he can tell they are nasty characters. The older female surveys the foxes with dead eyes. Something about her expression makes Shadow choke back a whimper, and he hunkers closer to the ground.

"So, Pennyroyal, have we reached an agreement?" The one-eyed coyote asks, grinning at the king of foxes.

"Indeed, we have, Thorn. Tonight, I will take you to the duck pond and show you all our best hunting places," Pennyroyal says evenly, maintaining steady eye contact with the leader of the coyotes.

Thorn turns his head to his mate and their pups and nods to them. They rise from their haunches in unison and draw closer to the trio of foxes. Shadow doesn't move a muscle. If he could bury himself in the ground, he would. But the coyotes fixate on Pennyroyal, Moon, and Mistletoe. They don't notice the little brown fox attempting to blend in with the green leaves of the cornstalks.

"Follow me," says Pennyroyal over his shoulder to the coyotes. All seven animals trot away from the scarecrow, toward the west, with Pennyroyal in the lead. Mistletoe is the last to follow. He looks back at Shadow momentarily, and cocking his head to the side, beckons the younger fox to follow. Shadow is afraid, but his curiosity wins out, and when the pack of coyotes and foxes are a safe distance away, he traces their path.

The animals lope on for a distance, clinging to the outskirts of Farmer Reynolds's property. In the distance, the white clapboard house looks cheery and welcoming with its windows lit from within. Shadow, who has never been so far away from the den by himself, marvels at everything with wonder. The night sky is luminous with stars, and each one seems to be spying on the little fox with wide eyes. Eventually, the pack of animals reach a marshy area with tall grass. A little way beyond, the water of a pond glistens in the moonlight. This is Farmer Reynolds's duck hunting pond. He goes here with Tomboy when Mrs. Reynolds has been particularly picky.

As the animals approach, a duck flies out of the grass on dark wings. Everyone stops, including Shadow, who makes himself small in the high grass flanking the pond.

"There are plenty of eggs and birds here to feed you and your family," Pennyroyal says, addressing Thorn.

Thorn surveys the pond, his one eye shining eerily in the night. "This will do for a night," he chuckles, turning to Pennyroyal and grinning fiercely. Pennyroyal regards him, his own face unchanging.

"There are nests of eggs on the other side of the pond," the leader of the foxes says, his voice quiet and steady. "We'll create a diversion for the ducks, and while they are distracted, you can go in and claim as many eggs as you want."

"What do we need you for? Surely, we know how

to hunt ducks," scoffs the one-eyed coyote's mate. Her eyes narrow, and she bares her teeth at Pennyroyal. From his hiding place in the tall grass, Shadow trembles at the sound of the female coyote's voice.

"Yes, I'm sure you do, but consider this an act of friendship, Nettle," Moon interjects. Nettle turns her attention to Pennyroyal's mate, a growl emanating from her mouth. As she lowers her head, Thorn steps in front of her.

"You may come along if you like," he laughs. "Perhaps you'll learn a few tricks watching coyotes hunt."

Pennyroyal turns to Moon and Mistletoe and looks at them meaningfully. Moon follows the bank of the pond to the left. Tall pines and some old fallen logs surround the duck pond. The other two foxes follow behind the coyotes. Shadow, who has gone undetected, follows along after as quietly as he can.

When they reach the other side of the pond, Moon stops and waits for the other animals to catch up with her. A few yards away stands a large tree with a hollow spot in its trunk. Moon glances at the tree, sniffing the air. She then turns to the rest of the animals there and addresses the coyotes.

"Pennyroyal, Mistletoe, and I will go and flush out the ducks for you, and you can go after their eggs untroubled."

The coyotes look back and forth at one another, snickering mildly. The foxes ignore their rude behavior and break up, each one disappearing into the tall grass around the pond. Shadow, who hasn't been discovered, feels a ripple of anticipation in the night air and doesn't move a muscle. Mistletoe appears in the tall grass next to his brother. Shadow almost yelps in surprise but manages to swallow down his voice when he recognizes his older brother.

"Come on, kid, we have someplace else to be, and things are about to get really hectic around here." Without another word, Mistletoe darts off into the grass away from the pond. Shadow, relieved not to have to hide anymore, chases after his brother in the moonlight.

Just as the two younger foxes speed off in search of their own adventure, a tumult of ducks take wing out of the grass into the dark sky, breaking the silence of the night. The coyotes are momentarily distracted watching the birds take flight. As the ducks ascend out of sight, a ferocious growl shatters the air around the coyotes.

Pennyroyal sprints out of the hollow tree. The coyotes stare at him as he rushes top speed through their ranks. In his wake, crashing and roaring like a tornado, Ursa the bear follows.

When she sees the coyotes, the bear bellows

a howl of fury, swiping at them left and right with her powerful paws. Her black fur blends into the darkness so she is merely a nightmare shadow, with only the gold of her eyes visible in her terrible face. The gang of coyotes scatter in separate directions. Disoriented, Ursa swipes blindly left and right, then barrels down after Nettle, who has stopped a little way off and is growling at the bear. Blind with fury, Ursa lumbers through the tall grass, up and away from the duck pond.

As the bear thunders after the female coyote, Thorn, Voodoo, and Ghost pull up behind Ursa, biting at her hind legs and deepening her rage. When she turns to attack one of her assailants, another attacks her from behind, utterly confusing her. She bellows once more in frustration, swiping at Voodoo, who deftly avoids the bear's deadly paws—only to be bitten in the hindquarters by Thorn, who seems to be enjoying the chase. Enraged, Ursa swipes at Nettle, who is back in front of her, growling and antagonizing the bear. Her paw lands with force on Nettle's torso, and the coyote goes rolling away into the tall grass. Startled, the other three coyotes close in on the bear, who is snarling and bristling with anger.

As the fight unfolds, Pennyroyal and Moon turn in the opposite direction, away from the duck pond and back toward the cornfield and the den.

"Where is Mistletoe?" Moon asks her mate as they run as fast as their legs can carry them.

"I saw him leaving the pond when I went into Ursa's lair," he reports between breaths. "And that's not all. Shadow was with him."

"Hurry up, Shadow! The stag is waiting for us," Mistletoe calls over his shoulder to his younger brother, who is struggling to keep up with the fast pace. Mistletoe feels alive with excitement. He didn't know what happened to the coyotes once the bear was roused, but whatever Ursa did wouldn't be sufficient to snuff out the threat that the foxes faced. He wishes his father would have listened to him, but none of that matters now. What's done is done. They must find Ahwi, the stag, and learn how to defeat the coyotes for good.

The two foxes enter the forest, their speed decreasing slightly as they dodge tree roots and undergrowth. Ahwi did not tell Mistletoe where in the forest he would find him, but Mistletoe suspects it must have something to do with the old oak tree with the strange, head-like growth that had frightened the brothers so much just a few days before. He makes his way through the woods, taking a different direction to avoid the pigs and their gallows humor.

"Hurry up, Shadow. We don't have much time," he calls over his shoulder to the younger fox.

Finally, they reach the clearing where the old oak tree stands. The moonlight dances off the gnarled branches, casting menacing shadows over the barren ground. As the brothers slowly approach, Ahwi, the mysterious stag, steps out from behind the tree. Both the foxes stop dead in their tracks, unsure of what to do next. They stare at Ahwi, who appears as big as a mountain to them. The enormous buck regards them with a deep, impenetrable gaze.

"Shadow, you are not welcome here. Only Mistletoe may enter." Ahwi's voice is resonant and absolute as he speaks. The two foxes cringe under the weight of his commandment, but neither moves a muscle.

"Ahwi, I meant no harm bringing Shadow. Please, tell me how to defeat the coyotes." Mistletoe addresses the great stag with reverence, but his voice contains a hint of defiance as well. As far as Mistletoe can tell, the foxes don't owe the stag anything—yet.

Ahwi says nothing. The two foxes exchange furtive glances between each other but say nothing. The moment seems to extend eternally, but after a brief pause, Ahwi speaks again. This time his voice is lower, almost a whisper.

"You must follow me into the tree. On the other

side, I will teach you what you desire to know." Again, Mistletoe and Shadow cast a look between them, questioning Ahwi's meaning. Tentatively, Mistletoe steps forward. As he does, the wind picks up, rustling the leaves of the forest eerily. The old oak tree sways slightly. Pausing, Mistletoe questions Ahwi.

"Why can't Shadow come with me? I don't want to leave him here alone." Mistletoe turns to look at his brother, whose eyes are wide with anticipation and fear.

"It is not his time yet," the stag says softly. Mistletoe turns back to Ahwi. The buck's eyes are full of age and wisdom and something that resembles sadness. The fox is so captivated that he momentarily forgets Shadow and his concerns for him.

The wind picks up a second time, and the fragile moment is lost. Mistletoe turns to his brother.

"Shadow, go back to the den. Find Mother and Father and tell them I am going to defeat the coyotes. Hurry. Go now!" His voice is gruff at the end, trying to bury his fear.

Shadow views his brother abruptly, as if forced out of a trance. When he hesitates, Mistletoe growls and shouts,

"Go now!" His brother's change in demeanor startles Shadow, so he scampers out of the clearing, his brown fur glimmering dully in the moonlight.

As Shadow hurries away, he hears a tremendous creaking and groaning coming from behind him in the clearing. Turning back, he catches a glimpse of the old oak tree, and the strange, head-like growth turning on its vine and springing to life. As the tree shakes and grinds its roots, the opening in the trunk appears, and the swirling void within is visible even to Shadow, who stares transfixed from the undergrowth just beyond the clearing. The space in the tree's trunk grows wider and wider and is soon so big it stands as tall as Ahwi, who is approaching the space slowly with Mistletoe beside him. The wind has begun to howl through the forest, and the tree's branches are thrashing from side to side. As Shadow chokes back a scream, the stag and the fox step into the chasm that has appeared in the oak's trunk.

And as Shadow watches, they disappear.

Chapter 9
THE OLD OAK TREE

The opening in the oak tree's trunk is black and smells of earth. Mistletoe's heart is hammering in his ears, but he walks boldly into the void, never flinching. When he is entirely within the tree, he looks back over his shoulder, hoping to catch a last glimpse of Shadow. But the opening he just walked through has disappeared. Surrounded by utter darkness, Mistletoe shudders involuntarily.

He has followed Ahwi into the opening in the tree, but now Mistletoe senses he is completely alone. He takes a breath—and then another. Before he can exhale a third time, the fox hears a voice coming to him from within the tree. It is not the stag's deep baritone, but rather a soft, feminine, musical voice.

"Mistletoe," it speaks, "follow the sound of my voice. I will lead you safely to the other side." As he listens, lights like shooting stars fall from above. Abruptly, Mistletoe feels himself falling. The lights dropping around him become brighter and quicker, changing colors and sparkling with intensity. Glowing ribbons of light soon surround the fox as he plummets.

"Don't be afraid. I am here," the disembodied voice whispers in his ear. Mistletoe can say nothing in return. The lights form into shapes and patterns that captivate the fox as though he is in a dream. Soon, Mistletoe can make out forms flowing past him on a river of light. As he watches, helpless, he recognizes scenes from his own life shining around him. First, he sees Shadow fleeing from the oak tree, back to the den, his eyes wild with fear. Next, the coyotes appear around him, fighting with Ursa the bear. He then sees images of himself, Pennyroyal, and Moon gathered around the scarecrow in the dying light. With each new visual memory, he experiences a flood of emotions that threaten to overwhelm him. He tries to scream, but no sound escapes. Only the images of his past, emerging rapidly, fill the space around him.

"Be at peace, Mistletoe," the voice utters softly. He continues to topple over himself, but the anxiety he felt has disappeared, replaced by a sense of calm and warmth. The scenes appearing in the river of light have changed. They are no longer events from Mistletoe's life, but rather images of another fox Mistletoe doesn't recognize. The fox looks older, wily, and he is loping through the woods along the Escatawpa River as though his life depends on it. As the scene unfolds, Mistletoe watches the old fox, wondering to himself who he could be. The old fox is dashing along the river of light, and then he stops, his long ears prickling to a sound he dreads. Mistletoe is helpless as he watches a hunter emerge from the forest, armed with a rifle, behind the magnificent fox. The hunter aims his gun, and the fox bows his head, as though surrendering to this last bit of cunning that has trumped his own. The shot fires, and the scene evaporates in the limitless void.

The young fox finds himself asleep in a meadow at dawn. As he blinks his weary eyes awake, he notices the dove hunting meadow near his parents' den along the towering pines. The air is sweet, and everything seems familiar, except it isn't. Something is different about the trees, the wind, and the cooing doves in the meadow. They all seem to be singing softly—and dancing. In harmony. Mistletoe furrows his brow. He faces the north, toward Farmer Reynolds's house—except it isn't there. He is certain he is in Farmer Reynolds's meadow, but where is Farmer Reynolds? The young fox rises to his feet and turns in a circle.

He remembers going into the tree with Ahwi, and he remembers visions of himself and another as though all a dream, but he doesn't recall how he got there. Before he can contemplate his lapse of memory too deeply, the world around him erupts into a joyous cacophony of song as the rosy fingers of dawn caress the meadow in golden light.

Everything is singing and dancing. The pines are swaying rhythmically, their slender branches and green needles fluttering gently, and Mistletoe swears he can see them smiling at him. The grass hums mindfully to itself, and every bird in the air is alive with songs of praise as they flit from tree to tree. In the sky, Dawn bends her lovely face down and reaches out to touch the face of the fox who is looking at her, his mouth agape. She smiles knowingly, her eyes full of kindness and hope, and continues on her path lighting up the world beyond.

Mistletoe is astounded. He has never known any world other than his own, let alone a magic world without Farmer Reynolds, and perhaps, all humans? The question is too broad for him to consider, so he sits back down in the grass, his jaw still unhinged, and watches the paradise around him.

After awhile of rest, the young fox rises to his feet again, stretches, and begins to walk. The grasses part gracefully before him as he wanders through this place so familiar, but at the same time so strange. The overwhelming chorus of dawn has meandered into a quiet choral arrangement among the day birds. Mistletoe listens to their symphony, mesmerized. He picks out different voices in the meadow. A doe—he can tell by her scent—sings among the pines, yards away from the fox. Her voice is calm and sweet, and she sings about the lovely day and the way of deer to her fawn.

And then, Mistletoe hears the voice that was speaking to him as he was falling through the void in the old oak tree. It is low and very beautiful. As it sings, praising the sun and its gifts, Mistletoe remembers everything that transpired on the river of light in his journey to the other side. He stops. The voice belongs to a female fox standing directly in front of him.

As foxes go, she is especially beautiful. She has lovely, deep auburn fur that glistens in the sunlight. Her eyes are pine-needle green, and the crest on her chest and the tip of her tail are so white, they dazzle Mistletoe's eyes as her tail waves lazily behind her. At first, neither creature speaks, and for a time on this bright, musical morning, the world seems to stand still. As though greeting an old friend, the vixen's face breaks into a radiant smile.

"Good morning, Mistletoe. I trust you slept well?" Her eyes are soft with kindness as she makes conversation.

"Who—who are you?" Mistletoe asks, dumbfounded. For the young fox, the events of the past few hours have seemed stranger and stranger. He cannot comprehend how this charming female fox knows who he is, and his curiosity has overcome his shyness. He anticipates that she will explain to him what's going on, but the pretty little vixen does something he hadn't expected—she throws back her head and laughs.

"Come on, silly," she teases over her shoulder, turning back the way she came. "You need a cool dip if you're to understand any of this." She regards Mistletoe, whose mouth has become permanently agape, and then trots away. Mistletoe hesitates, and then sighing, trots after her.

The mysterious vixen has begun to sing again. Mistletoe listens to her song, and after a while, finds himself humming along to her melody.

As Dawn approaches in the sky,
I watch my spirit flow away.
Awaken world with sunny rays,
We gather round to sing her praise.

As they walk along, Mistletoe notices the birds. They are performing aerial acrobatics, perfectly synchronized and gorgeous in their symmetry. Their song aligns with their flight of dance, building toward a brilliant crescendo as birds circle and burst through the light clouds skimming across the glowing sky. The deer and her fawn have retreated into the forest, and the two foxes are alone in the meadow, save for the chorus of birds overhead and the trees swaying to the tune Mistletoe's companion sings.

The two continue on a path that would lead them to Farmer Reynolds's farmhouse, except of course, it isn't there. The barn and the chickens are nowhere. Mistletoe remembers just yesterday he was hiding among Mrs. Reynolds's roses, trying to find the noisy raven Francis and get him to keep his big beak shut. Now, nothing is there except verdant, lush grass. Soon, the pair are where the cornfield should be, but again, it is just meadow and a copse of trees.

The mysterious vixen has stopped singing, and the two resume in silence, except for the very air around them seeming alive with a wild sense of joy. Mistletoe is so enchanted by the new world around him, he has momentarily forgotten where he comes from and why he is there. The coyotes are a faint memory to him, the threat they present a distant storm that the young fox can easily dismiss as he watches the trees sighing in the glory of the sun.

Eventually, the two foxes come to the duck pond. As they approach, Mistletoe feels a growing sense of unease, although the light on the water is fantastic, and the ducks swimming lazily in the water barely notice the predators as they approach. One great big mallard with a red crest on his head even greets Mistletoe with a warm hello, to which the surprised fox returns a feeble greeting. He has never been acknowledged by prey before in any other way than fear, and the duck seems so content to share the pond with the fox that Mistletoe sits down abruptly, his black feet giving out from under him. He remembers the events of the night before and how he abandoned his family to follow a magical stag, go through a time warp, and be a hero. Ashamed of himself, he lays his head on his forepaws, watching the ducks glide along the surface of the pond in an artistic formation.

Just as Mistletoe is beginning to really feel sorry for himself, the little vixen gallops past him at top speed. Reaching the edge of the pond, she launches herself into the air, tucks her legs and tail up, and hits the water in a forceful cannonball dive. Water spills from the pond, utterly drenching the poor fox sitting meekly on the shore. Startled, Mistletoe shakes droplets from his ears and whiskers and looks stonily at the other fox, who is laughing heartily as she swims on her back.

"Come on, Mistletoe. The water is great!" she exclaims, an enormous grin on her face. Mistletoe rises to his feet, his jaw working back and forth as he contemplates his companion. The young fox is still chagrined about the part he has played in this new adventure, but for now, he is willing to cast his doubts aside to learn more about this peculiar vixen and the world she lives in.

"What's your name?" he queries, figuring the direct approach is the best one. The little fox in the water views him from the side as she joins the ducks, who are now bobbing and diving in the water in a delicate pattern. She dives down with the ducks, and when she resurfaces, she shoots a stream of water from her mouth at Mistletoe, again drenching his ears and whiskers.

"Dogwood," she finally replies, laughing as the young fox shakes his head vigorously to rid himself of the water.

"Well, Dogwood," Mistletoe's voice has an edge of annoyance, "how do you know my name without me even telling you?" He eyes the little vixen suspiciously, ducking his head as she produces another fountain of water from her gurgling mouth.

"I've always known you," Dogwood murmurs, and her eyes are suddenly so innocent and truthful that Mistletoe can't help but believe her, even though he has never met her until today. Perplexed, Mistletoe sits back down again on his haunches and allows one black forepaw to trace ripples in the pond as he ponders what this could possibly mean. For her part, Dogwood seems to have momentarily forgotten her befuddled friend and has started singing again, gazing at the sky from her back in the water.

As Mistletoe regards the pond, he notices that the water has changed. Whereas when they arrived, the water was so clear the bottom was perfectly visible, now it has begun to swirl and darken around the young fox's paw. Mistletoe furrows his brow as he watches—it looks as though images appear in the water.

After a few moments, the images become clearer. He sees the duck pond, but this time a group of animals are fighting around it. Mistletoe recognizes his parents, Pennyroyal and Moon, and the coyotes. Among them, Ursa the bear swings her powerful forelegs at the coyotes, slapping the one called Nettle away. In turn, the vicious gang attack the bear, biting her and causing her to bellow. Eventually, as Mistletoe watches, he sees the coyotes bring the bear down at the edge of the cornfield. Their attack is brutal and without mercy. Transfixed, the young fox sees his parents escaping from the carnage and gazes helplessly as the water muddies, then clears, a new vision appearing in the liquid pool. He sees Shadow speeding away from the oak tree, back to the den like Mistletoe told him. Only, as he watches, the two younger coyotes intercept Shadow, blocking his progress through the forest.

Mistletoe wants to scream at his brother to leave, but the vision in the pond merely shows the three animals trotting off together before the water clears again, and the scene disappears.

"What's happened to them?" he asks Dogwood frantically, who has swum back to where Mistletoe sits on the shore. She emerges from the water, and her face is very pensive.

"You are here because of them, Mistletoe, but the time has not come yet," Dogwood replies cryptically, her expression unreadable.

Mistletoe is pacing back and forth along the water's edge, his body almost vibrating with fearful energy. He can't understand what is happening or what Dogwood could possibly mean by her strange reply of not being ready yet. He knows he must get back to his world somehow, but he is so confused he can't make a decision. *What is happening to Shadow? Why did he leave with the coyotes?* Mistletoe is wracked with questions he cannot answer and which Dogwood doesn't seem to want to. The two regard one another for a long moment, and then a cheerful voice comes from behind.

"Dogwood? Is that you? Well, how are you this fine morning?" Both foxes turn to see a little rabbit sitting on its haunches, a broad grin blooming across its face.

Chapter 10

THE OTHER SIDE

"Pansy?" Dogwood exclaims, right before she lunges at the little rabbit who has greeted her in such a friendly manner. Mistletoe's heart is thumping in his ears as he watches her, expecting Dogwood to go in for the kill. Instead, the two fall on each other, wrestling playfully in the tall grass next to the pond and giving each other affectionate licks on the nose. Bewildered, Mistletoe shifts nervously side to side as he watches the two friends. He has never known a world without Farmer Reynolds, and he has certainly never known a world where a fox and a rabbit are friends. Watching them at their play, the fox momentarily forgets the vision of Shadow and the two younger coyotes and laughs.

"What's the matter, Mistletoe? Haven't you ever seen a fox and a rabbit who are best friends before?" Dogwood smiles affectionately at the young fox, winking at him as Pansy falls back in the grass, her forelegs crossed behind her long fuzzy ears.

"I am a very sophisticated rabbit—I only consort with the finest of creatures. Good to meet you, Mistletoe!" Pansy chitters, as Dogwood flops down next to the rabbit. Finally, Mistletoe drops down in the grass after them, utterly bemused. The three lay on their backs, watching the slender clouds skid across the sky and listening to the music the ducks make as they splash in the pond.

"What is this place?" Mistletoe asks quietly, almost to himself. The vixen and rabbit regard him, then each other. A knowing look passes between them, but Mistletoe's two companions say nothing, and the three lapse into silence once again.

After a time, Dogwood rises to her feet and looks down on the fox and rabbit. This time, Pansy and Mistletoe exchange a look, then, without warning, both spring at the vixen at the same time, jumping on her back and pushing her to the ground. Surprised, Dogwood rolls out from under her assailants and flees away from the pond toward the forest. Delighted, Mistletoe and Pansy give chase. Soon, all three animals are under the cool canopy of the woods.

Everything is a brilliant green—the colors are so vivid the leaves glow like emeralds on the trees. The two foxes meander through the woods slowly with Pansy hopping along lazily behind. Here, the song of the day is softer and more subdued, but even still, Mistletoe can hear the trees humming a tune in complex harmony. The three animals remain quiet as they listen.

Eventually, the companions come to the waters of Big Creek rushing through the forest. Here, the bubbling water is singing a song of its own, weaving through the voices of the trees. Mistletoe sits down to listen, and Dogwood and Pansy stand on either side of him, looking down the embankment at the water. Just yesterday, Mistletoe was chasing a rabbit alongside the creek when he met Ahwi the stag, who initiated this whole adventure. But today, the other embankment is empty, save for the trees singing their sleepy chorus. Disappointed, Mistletoe remains sitting with the other two creatures beside him.

"What's wrong?" Pansy asks the sighing fox. Mistletoe peers at the little rabbit. She turns her head to look at him with her blue eye, the pupil expanding as she contemplates her large red companion. Her pink nose quivers slightly as she sniffs the air, reading the fox's emotions by his scent. In the distance, a faint peal of thunder ripples over the air.

"Nothing," Mistletoe replies, and he grins at Pansy. "This place is…beautiful." Mistletoe lands on the word clumsily, unable to think of a way to describe what he is feeling to the little rabbit. He hesitates, then says sheepishly, "I want to know where I am and why I am here."

Pansy and Dogwood exchange another look, then Dogwood nods and leaps quickly away into the forest. Startled, Mistletoe rises to his feet, scanning the undergrowth leading out from the creek for a sight of her as the music of the trees goes on uninterrupted. He jumps again when he feels the rabbit's paw on his shoulder. But before he can whirl on this peculiar hare, her soft voice consoles him, and he can feel her pet his fur.

"There, there," she comforts him with feeling. "You're in Alabama."

As the fox and rabbit walk along with one another, Pansy tells Mistletoe about her world.

"In the beginning, the Great Creator only created our one world, yours and mine together. But when First Fox lost his magic and First Man began hunting the animals for food and for sport, the one world split apart. At first, the world had only split a little. Both sides were the same, like a mirror reflection, and a creature could go from one to the other without batting an eye. But as First Man's greed grew, the crack deepened, and it became impossible for any animals caught on the other side to get back over, or vice versa. Only one can cross from one side to the other, and that is Ahwi, the stag you followed into the tree."

"So, you know Ahwi? Please, tell me where to find him." Mistletoe, who had begun to relax after Dogwood's abrupt departure, nervously bounces on his black feet and frantically searches around.

Pansy stops walking and simply watches the fox as he circles his flame-colored body around and around, his ears twitching in different directions as though listening for the stag. When he realizes the little rabbit is no longer beside him, he looks back down the path they've been traveling and sees her sitting there. Chagrined, he trots back to where she is. Another rumble of thunder echoes over the clouds, closer now.

"As I was saying, Ahwi is the only one who can travel between the worlds. Mostly, he just watches. But sometimes, he must intervene." Pansy pauses and looks meaningfully at Mistletoe. "And he will find you when you are ready."

"What does that mean, when I am ready?" Mistletoe casts a glance down at the gray hare who is hopping softly alongside of him. She has been trying to explain things to him, but he is more confused than ever. Two worlds? A magic stag who can leap between them? He has more questions now than ever before, but he doesn't want to anger the little rabbit. She may be small, but something in her demeanor makes Mistletoe think she can be a tough old bird when she wants to be.

Pansy lets out a peal of laughter, thumping her left foot twice on the ground. As she does, a sudden summer rain shower stirs the air overhead, drenching the poor fox for the second time that day. Again, she giggles, and thumping her long foot once, the storm blows away, leaving nothing but pure sunshine in its wake.

"All the animals here have their own magic, Mistletoe. I expect Ahwi will find you when you have found yours."

Sometime while Mistletoe and Pansy make their way back through the forest, Dogwood rejoins them, panting heavily with a huge grin plastered across her face.

"I wish y'all could have seen it," she stammers between breaths. "Butterflies everywhere! So many colors, and they were all dancing in the field." She playfully collapses in the foliage of ferns, her pink tongue lolling out of the side of her mouth. "They asked me to dance, and I couldn't keep up!"

"That's because you don't have wings," Pansy says evenly, rolling her eyes at Mistletoe and making him smirk.

The sun is moving lower in the sky, and as dusk approaches, the planet Venus rises with her crown of light above the darkening tree line. The three animals watch as the sky changes colors, and their own features become more subdued in the growing darkness.

As the sun sinks lower, Pansy detaches herself from her companions, and turning to them with an iridescent glow in her eyes, she says, "I must depart from you now, Dogwood and Mistletoe. Night is upon us, and Thistle will wonder where I am." She nods to the foxes, and with a flourish of her cottony tail, leaps off into the twilight, leaving the young fox and the vixen alone together.

"Who is Thistle?" Mistletoe asks shyly, suddenly self-conscious left alone with such a pretty vixen. Dogwood looks at Mistletoe, and in the dying light, he can see that she is still smiling at him.

"He's her mate," she says, and without warning, she pounces on the unsuspecting fox, knocking the wind out of him as she pins him to the ground.

"Hey! Hold on a minute," he grunts, pushing the little red vixen off him. As her feet hit the ground, she darts like a shadow through the trees with only the white tip of her tail visible in the darkness. Without thinking, Mistletoe gives chase, and the two foxes dance together in the nighttime forest, laughing and tumbling among the bushes.

Eventually, the pair make their way to the duck pond. The sun has fully set behind the trees, and the black sky is a map of stars reflected in the still water. Dogwood enters the pond first, with Mistletoe submerging himself behind her. Their red fur appears black in the dark water, and as they swim, the reflection of starlight illuminates their bodies. In contrast to the music of the day, Mistletoe notices that a blanket of peaceful silence seems to cover everything—the only sound the gentle lapping of water at the bank of the pond and the frogs croaking for their mates.

The two swim together quietly for some time, ducking and diving in the cool water. Dogwood dives down, and when she doesn't resurface, Mistletoe is worried and swims in circles, scanning the dark bottom for his friend. Finally, the playful vixen shoots out from the depths of the pond like an arrow, arcing through the air and landing with a tremendous belly flop back in the water next to Mistletoe, who tries to avoid her undertow. She expertly swims to her companion and placing her two front paws on the top of his head, pushes him under the surface. When Mistletoe bobs back up, he is coughing as water spews from his mouth. Perturbed, he swims away, his back to Dogwood. Not wanting to offend, she swims fast behind him, intending to apologize, but as she draws close enough to whisper in his ear, the wily fox spins around and dunks her head beneath the water. Laughing, the two foxes swim back to the shore, flopping down between the cattails.

"This morning, you said you had always known me. How can that be? I've never been here before." Mistletoe looks sideways at the little fox next to him, beads of water on her whiskers glittering in the starlight. He doesn't want to annoy her, but he must get answers to his questions. The memory of Shadow and the coyotes has not entirely left him, and if finding out as much as he can about this place will help him to complete his quest, he will ask as many questions as it takes. Plus, he is curious.

Dogwood returns Mistletoe's gaze with such a loving look that the bashful boy fox must look away. Sighing at his reluctance, she lays her head on her forepaws and gazes up at the luminous night sky.

"When the one world split into two, several of the animals were caught on the other side." She looks down at the pond. "When it first happened, many of the animals were able to come back. But some remained trapped and couldn't use their magic. As the world split further, Man moved completely into your world because the animals had no way of defending themselves and it made hunting easier. The chasm deepened, and numerous animals were lost. Those of us who stayed on this side lost friends, and parents, and mates." At this last statement, Dogwood swallows hard. "But when Ahwi came and could see what was happening on the other side, he promised that the ones we had lost would come back to us." She beholds Mistletoe, and a silent message passes between the two animals, who are so captivated with one another.

The young fox, who has listened attentively to her story, falls into her eyes, which are glowing with night shine and sadness. She is so lovely and sweet, and her words are so earnest. Mistletoe has never known love before, but as he watches his courageous, silly companion, he feels something new and hopeful blossoming in his heart. The two lean together, affectionately rubbing their heads.

Just then, a great shadow appears over the water of the two lovers. Ahwi, the great stag, towers above them. Mistletoe and Dogwood jump to their feet beneath Ahwi's antlered head.

"The time is here, Mistletoe. Come with me." And without a word, the young fox walks off with the giant buck, leaving Dogwood, a flame-colored vixen, alone on the shore of the duck pond.

Chapter 11
SHADOW AND THE BEAR

As soon as he sees Mistletoe disappear into the old oak tree, Shadow speeds back to the den as fast as his legs can carry him. He gets wet crossing one of the streams from the artesian well, but even this does not slow him down. All he can think of is reaching his parents and telling them about Mistletoe and the stag. He hopes that Pennyroyal and Moon are all right after rousing the bear and that Ursa has done her job driving the coyotes from their territory. As he races along, he remembers all the events leading up to this moment, especially the terrifying gang of coyotes. He recalls the voice of the one-eyed leader's mate, and another shiver dances down his spine.

Just before Shadow reaches the tree line separating the forest from Farmer Reynolds's dove hunting meadow, two dark forms emerge from behind a giant pine and block the little brown fox's path. As the forms draw closer, Shadow can make out the younger coyotes from the gang—the offspring of Thorn and his mate, Nettle. Shadow stops, and turning, tries to escape the other way, except the coyotes are instantly there, preventing him from proceeding. He stops again, and this time, he doesn't move.

"What's a little fox like you doing out so late without your chaperone?" The female coyote says menacingly.

"Come now, Voodoo, give him a break. He was just waiting to talk to us alone," the male coyote taunts, smiling between razor sharp teeth. The two coyotes exchange a look and then laugh. Shadow shivers, hunching lower to the ground and baring his teeth. When the predators see the little fox snarling at them, they both let out a guffaw.

"What do you think you're going to do, little kit?" The one called Voodoo says to him. She circles close to Shadow, brushing against him. When her body touches his, Shadow lets out an involuntary yelp. The two coyotes resume their snickering.

"We saw you in the cornfield," the male coyote says, yawning theatrically. "We think the three of us can have some fun together tonight." He turns to Shadow, his eyes bright and malicious. Shadow recoils, but there is nowhere for him to run.

"What a fabulous idea!" Voodoo says animatedly to her brother. "I'm in the mood to hunt some chickens. How about you, Ghost?"

"I'd like nothing better," Ghost growls. "Whaddya say, Shadow? Are you in the mood to hunt some chickens?" The coyote's face is inches from the little fox's, and Shadow can feel Ghost's hot breath on his muzzle. It smells of Ursa the bear and blood.

"No! We're not allowed to hunt the chickens!" Shadow shouts. He almost chokes on the words; he is so terrified. Voodoo and Ghost both narrow their eyes at him, their heads down and the fur on their spines bristling. They can sense his fear, and it excites them.

"Sure, you are," whispers Voodoo, her voice full of mock tenderness. "Think how happy your parents will be when you bring them back a fine, fat chicken. Quite the hunter, they'll say." Again, the two coyotes snigger as they regard the shivering little fox.

"Come on, Shadow. We'll talk about how proud your parents will be as we go," Ghost says. The two coyotes flank the brown fox. He rises to his feet, and the three animals walk out of the forest together into the dove hunting meadow.

When the trio come to the fence separating the meadow from Farmer Reynolds's yard, Shadow attempts to make a break for it. Before he gets a yard, however, Voodoo is on top of him, pinning him to the ground with her forelegs, her teeth at his throat.

"Try and run again and you're dead, fox," she growls. Shadow stays motionless. When Voodoo finally releases him, Shadow realizes with a growing sense of humiliation that he has wet himself. The coyotes can smell his embarrassment and shake their heads in disgust.

"No more running, and no more accidents. Our mother took a beating because of your parents." At this, Ghost slaps the little fox, leaving a trail of scratches across his nose. "We intend to pay them back in kind."

At the mention of his parents, Shadow feels a stirring in his spirit, and the fear of the moment drops away as he musters his courage. After all, Mistletoe isn't the only hero in the family.

"Bet you can't hunt chickens as well as a fox can." Shadow gives Ghost a long, defiant look, then darts under the wooden fence beam straight toward the chicken coop. Laughing and whooping, the two coyotes follow suit.

As they near the chicken coop, Voodoo and Ghost lapse into a deadly silence. Shadow spots them, and notices that they have split up and are now at either side of the coop. Swallowing down a huge lump in his throat, Shadow tiptoes up the ramp leading to the chicken house.

Just before dawn, in the darkest part of the night, Shadow can't hear anything except the blood thrumming in his own ears. He can smell the sleeping chickens inside the opening to the coop and hopes the hammering of his heart doesn't wake the biddies. Shadow has never hunted anything larger than a beetle by himself before, but instinct tells him that silence is his friend.

When he enters the dark doorway and is inside the coop, the smell of the hens is so overpowering, Shadow starts to salivate. He looks to the right and to the left, and realizes he is surrounded by sleeping chickens—about fifteen. Lowering his head, he spots a white broody hen snoozing away, her narcissistic head drooping to the side. The fox parts his lips and slinks his way over to his unsuspecting prey.

Just as Shadow opens his jaws to clamp down on the neck of the sleeping chicken, her eyes pop open, and she lets out an enormous squawk as the entire coop springs to life with terrified, noisy chickens. The alarmed fox whirls around. The coyotes are barking and yelping and tearing the hens' nests out from under them until they finally bolt out the door, each with a dead hen in their mouth. Before Shadow can follow them, the scared birds descend from their destroyed clutches and peck at him mercilessly.

Finally, Shadow manages to escape the startled

chickens and their attack. He scrambles down the ramp of the coop into the yard. Voodoo and Ghost are gone. What the little brown fox does see, however, is the angry face of Tomboy, Farmer Reynolds's black Lab, snarling at him, and Farmer Reynolds himself, standing in his pajamas with his shotgun pointed straight at Shadow. A flashlight on the ground illuminates the scene.

"Such a little fox to cause all this commotion. He must be starving," Farmer Reynolds mutters to himself, closing one eye as he takes aim. Shadow is frozen where he stands outside the coop, his eyes shining silver and gold in the light from the flashlight. He stares at the farmer and unconsciously matches his breath to the man's. The man and the fox inhale, and in the distance, an owl screeches a warning as the man squeezes the trigger. At the same time, Tomboy begins barking ferociously, her gray muzzle pointed toward the dove hunting meadow. Distracted, Farmer Reynolds misses his shot, instead hitting the dirt a few feet in front of the fox. Before he can reload, Shadow, as though waking from a trance, bolts into the darkness and the cornfield beyond.

He dashes, quick as lightning, through the cornfield. He is so disoriented from the night's events, he can't remember which direction the den is in. The leaves of the corn are thick and obscuring, but

Shadow doesn't slow down. Fear has taken hold, and the little brown fox feels that he will run until his legs fall off or he finds the edge of the world, whichever comes first.

As morning approaches, he comes to an abrupt stop, panting and shaking with sobs. He wishes he had never left Mistletoe or the den. He misses his parents and his sisters. *What will happen to them?* He was never able to tell them what happened with the stag, and the tree, and his brother. And that Mistletoe said he would be back and know how to defeat the coyotes. Knowing he failed his mission, Shadow sinks to the earth between the rows of corn, the weight of shame pressing him down.

While on the ground, weeping, Shadow hears a faint moaning coming from some rows over in the field. Rising to his feet, the little fox perks his ears to the sound and commences weaving his way through the cornstalks in search of the owner of the voice he hears.

The bear lies on her side in the cornfield, her fur mottled with blood and her ribs exposed. She is dying, and Shadow stops when he sees her. The bear can sense someone is there, and fearing her attackers, she swings her wounded head around to look in the direction of Shadow's footsteps. Catching sight of the little fox, she faintly bellows at him.

Shadow makes no movement. Filled with compassion, he forgets his own shame as he looks at the majestic animal lying helpless on the ground. He knows his father meant the bear no harm when he pitted her against the coyotes, but Shadow now knows that Pennyroyal underestimated Thorn and his gang—badly. He tries to convey his sorrow to the bear with his eyes, afraid that speaking to her will upset her and cause her more pain. Her own eyes are full and speak of sorrow and something wild and untamed. They seem to say that she is proud of how she fought and will die. The pair gaze at one another as the sun ascends her throne in the sky.

When the sky is fully light, the bear turns her head away from Shadow and breathes her last. Realizing that she is gone, Shadow approaches her body and nuzzles the powerful head and paws, pausing between each to look again into the now lifeless eyes. The only sound is the rustling of the cornstalk leaves in the wind.

He stays by the bear's body until Farmer Reynolds's truck climbs the road that surrounds the cornfield. Knowing that Tomboy will lead the man to this spot, Shadow nuzzles the bear's head one last time and takes off in the direction of the forest. He knows where he is and can find his way back to the den.

As he walks through the green woods, he thinks

back over the night's adventures. He wonders, if the coyotes saw him in the cornfield with his family when he was hiding, how much else they saw. He also wonders what it means that Tomboy and the farmer saw him outside the chicken coop. Surely, they will have noticed the missing chickens Voodoo and Ghost ran off with and will blame him for it. Shadow shakes his head, the thoughts overwhelming him.

He stops to eat some berries. The fruit is sweet and reminds him of his hunger. He sits in the dappled light of the sun streaming through the leaves, picking berries off the vine and chewing them thoughtfully. He eats until he is full, then wanders back through the trees in the direction of the den.

When he reaches the tree line, Shadow bounds forward. He can see the dove hunting meadow and the den beyond it. He is so excited to see his family, he doesn't notice the shadow eclipsing his own until he looks behind and sees the huge one-eyed coyote coming down on him like thunder.

"Not so fast," Thorn orders, batting the little brown fox to the ground with his paw.

Chapter 12

THE FARMER

Farmer Reynolds curses under his breath when he misses his shot. Grimacing at Tomboy, the man heads to the destroyed chicken coop, leaning his gun against its wall. He sticks his head inside and pulls the chain that connects to an exposed overhead light. The clutches are in disarray, with broken eggs and bedding littering the floor. Some of the chickens have gone back to sleep, while the others are rustling about the coop, pecking each other and fluttering their wings restlessly. Two of the chickens are missing.

Farmer Reynolds sighs to himself and rubs his brow with his thumb and forefinger. He can hardly believe the small fox, no more than a kit, was responsible for this much damage. But the farmer—who is no longer a young man—has seen too many strange things from the animal kingdom to put much thought into how the fox managed to do it. Instead, the old farmer must devise a plan to protect his chickens from further attacks. And that means setting traps for the foxes.

Tomboy is still barking with agitation in the direction of the meadow. She is getting older, and her ability to predict the farmer's movements are weakening. *Soon, she'll just be a porch dog and will retire from hunting. But not yet.* Her gray muzzle resembles his own, and the thought of not having the dog at his right hand makes him feel as though he is losing a piece of himself. He will simply have to be more diligent when it comes time to hunt.

"Hush now, girl," the man says softly to the black Lab, quieting her. She turns to her master, and the two share a warm, understanding look that puts the farmer in a better mood than the one he was in a few moments ago. Dawn is approaching, and the farmer picks up his rifle and walks back to the house to get dressed and tell Mrs. Reynolds about the chicken coop.

In their bedroom, he changes into faded blue overalls, heavy work boots, and a thin white T-shirt. Mrs. Reynolds is aghast as her husband tells her about the destroyed nests and the missing chickens. She sits up in their oak bed, her curlers drooping over her lined forehead and her mouth tight as she listens to the news.

"But George, what are we going to do? A fox can wipe out all our hens!" she exclaims, an edge of a whine entering her voice. She peers at her husband, this man she has shared a bed and a life with for fifty-some years, trying to read his face. So many years, and yet still strangers in so many ways. Farmer Reynolds sighs.

"Don't worry, June. I have a plan," he responds, keeping his back to his wife as he ties the laces on his boots. He can feel her eyes trained on him, and for a moment he feels caught, like an animal by a hunter.

He relaxes, exhaling deeply when she lets out an appreciative cluck, replying, "Yes, George. I trust you." She swings her veiny legs out from under the covers and plants her withered feet onto the hardwood floor.

After dressing, Farmer Reynolds descends the stairs and walks to the kitchen, where he makes himself a cup of coffee. The sliver of yesterday's moon is just cresting over the trees, and like so many mornings, the old farmer stands at the back screen door facing the barn, admiring the pale pinks and yellows of the clouds touched by the early sun. When he has finished his cup, he descends the three steps to the yard and heads toward the barn.

The weather is hot, humid, and the farmer can sense a storm brewing. He must hurry if he's to lay the traps before it rains. Still, there are chores to be completed. Inside the barn, he flicks on the lights, greeting the trio of cows ready to be milked. The farmer has eschewed milking machines in favor of doing it by hand—the way he learned when he was a boy. Besides, he is an expert milker and can have all the cows finished in under forty minutes. Sitting down at the first cow, a sweet little Jersey named Betsy, he pats her on the side before reaching under her to begin milking.

When he has finished all three cows, he rises to his feet slowly, placing his hand on the stall for balance. He has been feeling his age lately, and this makes him angry. Damned if he can't do everything he used to, and more. Still, his back hurts more than usual, and he finds himself at the coffee pot more and more throughout the day to keep his energy up. Dr. Robison has told him repeatedly he needs to slow down. *Just like Tomboy.* He chuckles to himself at the thought of the old, determined dog. He'll slow down—eventually. But not today. He lets the cows out into the grazing pasture and then walks back to the house.

Normally, Farmer Reynolds would take his tractor to check his crops, but today he needs to go to town, so he will take the pickup truck. Popping his head through the front door to retrieve his shotgun where he left it, he calls out a farewell to his wife.

"Load up, girl," he shouts, whistling for Tomboy, and gets into the blue Ford after the black dog jumps in ahead of him. The old truck cranks to life with a couple of tries, and the farmer pulls into reverse, his freckled arm on the seat behind Tomboy's head. Shifting gears, he exits the driveway, picking up the dirt road leading out to the northwestern side of his property and the cornfields. It is time to check on the western side of the crop growing adjacent to his duck hunting pond. He thinks he may go fishing later if the weather holds out. The thought of casting his line into the water calms him from the agitation he has been feeling about the chicken coop and the fox.

George Reynolds's father taught him to hunt when he was still a young boy, but his father had also taught him that everything in nature deserves respect and to never kill unless it was absolutely necessary—either to feed your family or to save your life and property. The farmer took this lesson to heart and had been profoundly disturbed when he saw the brown fox kit outside the hen house. The elder had grown accustomed to watching from a distance the foxes dart from their den to the meadow and the surrounding woods. Initially, when the fox family moved onto the property, Mrs. Reynolds had wrung her hands about the safety of the chickens. But it had been years since the sleek red animals had made their appearance, and the chickens had remained safe—until this morning.

Still, the farmer intends to purchase no-kill traps in town after checking the crops. What he'll do with the animals once they are caught, he'll figure out later. Probably drive them over the state line and drop them in Mississippi. Let them be that state's problem.

When the man and his dog approach the western portion of the cornfield, Tomboy barks aggressively. Her hackles are up, and she is halfway out the passenger side window. Farmer Reynolds stops the pickup and cuts the engine. As he does, Tomboy scrambles out of the window and leaps to the ground, like a dog half her age. She darts off between the rows of corn, barking, so that the farmer has to jog to keep up with her. When she finally stops, the farmer sees what has the dog so riled up. A dead bear lies on the ground, her hide ripped open and several cornstalks crushed beneath her tremendous weight. Around the carcass, in the soft dirt, are animal footprints; some belonging to the bear, others belonging to several dog-like animals, although Farmer Reynolds suspects it was not a pack of dogs that did this.

Realizing he has left his gun in the truck, he whistles for Tomboy, who reluctantly returns to him, and the two walk briskly back to the Ford to retrieve the shotgun. The farmer doubts that whoever did this is still hanging around, but he is a man of caution, preferring to prepare for all eventualities. When the pair return to the bear, the man examines the tracks more closely, bending down with effort to trace his finger along the edge of the paw prints. They are too large to be fox prints, and the farmer simply cannot believe that even a whole slew of foxes could bring down a bear. No, these tracks belong to coyotes; he is almost certain of it.

Coyotes were introduced into Alabama by hunters back in the 1930s, and Farmer Reynolds has occasionally encountered one in the woods over the years growing up in Big Creek, but he's never seen one on his property before, let alone a pack of them. Frowning, the man stands back up, and turning his attention to the bear, determines how he will dispose of it. He has a tarp and some rope in the bed of the pickup, so hauling the body won't be too much trouble, but he already knows he's going to have to burn the carcass, so that's one more thing he'll have to do today. Fishing is definitely out. Besides, he has a worse problem. If a pack of coyotes are on his property, that could spell disaster for his livestock. He'll still have to pick up the traps for the foxes—he'll never hear the end of it from Mrs. Reynolds if he doesn't—but this new turn of events will require nighttime vigils with his gun, driving and walking the perimeter of his property.

As he walks back to the pickup to unload the rope and tarp, he wonders again about the little fox standing transfixed outside the chicken coop. Is it possible that the coyotes are responsible for the damage to his property and the missing hens? Grabbing his work gloves, he questions if the foxes and coyotes may be working together but dismisses the idea as fanciful.

Back on the road, with the dead bear under the tarp and tied down in the bed of the truck, Farmer Reynolds turns north onto Grand Bay Road that heads into the town of Big Creek and further on until it meets with Airport Boulevard in Mobile. Today, he is only going as far as the town and the couple of stores that flank what Big Creek calls a main street. His first stop is at the grain and feed store, where he picks up supplies to help rebuild the hen's destroyed clutches. Tomboy waits patiently in the cab of the truck as the farmer makes his way inside the store. Jim, the owner, is not there today, so Farmer Reynolds grabs what he came for and doesn't stay to chat.

When he has loaded the bags of chicken feed and straw into the bed of the pickup, pushing the bear as much to the side as he can, he crosses the street to the hardware store to pick up the traps. While he is in the checkout lane, he gets to talking to Bill, the man who owns the farm to the south of his own.

"Bill, you'll never believe what I've got out in my pickup."

"What's that, George?"

"A dead bear. Found her in the cornfield this morning. I'm thinking coyotes mighta done it."

"Coyotes? Around here?" At this, Bill lifts his eyebrows at his friend.

"Sure, Bill. You know how them critters migrate. Anything's possible."

"Of course, anything's possible." Bill shrugs as though acquiescing to Farmer Reynolds's wisdom on these matters. "Is that what the traps are for?"

"No." Farmer Reynolds relays the events of early this morning to his friend; he was roused from bed by Tomboy's barking only to find a tiny, terrified fox kit outside the chicken coop.

"Sounds like you have one big problem, George," Bill says, chewing his thumbnail thoughtfully.

The farmer grunts, leaves the line, and rolls his buggy to the back of the store. When he returns, he pays for the merchandise, shakes Bill's hand, and the two men part ways.

Back on the road, the farmer stops at the gas station where they sell the local honey Mrs. Reynolds likes so much and picks up a jar for her. *If she didn't have honey, she'd be no sweeter than a thumbtack.* He feels ashamed for thinking of his wife that way. He remembers when they first met, and how pretty she was, and her lilting laughter at all his jokes, even the terrible ones. He smiles at the memory of them fishing the sweet tea waters of the Escatawpa River when they first got together and how she purposely capsized the boat. As he drives, he hums a little tune to himself, turning back on the dirt road that heads to home, and to her.

Chapter 13

TOMBOY

When the pickup truck returns to the farm, Tomboy exits the passenger side and goes in search of Ruby. The cat was sleeping at the foot of the Reynolds's bed when the chickens were attacked early this morning, and she didn't bother to see what the commotion was despite Tomboy's furious barking.

Now midday, the old black Lab heads in the direction of the porch. Ruby typically is there at this time, her languid body stretched lazily across the floorboards. As Tomboy approaches, she spies the cat's mottled fur glistening in a ray of sun. Ruby is curled up in Mrs. Reynolds's porch rocker, snoozing blissfully. The old dog snorts with annoyance as she walks painfully up the front steps.

"Well, I see you're doing what you do best," Tomboy mutters.

Ruby slowly opens one green eye, then the other. Then she stretches her body out, yawning luxuriously. Tomboy stares at the cat coldly as she begins grooming her fur with her tongue.

When she has finished giving herself a bath, she looks over at the Lab and purrs, "Problems?" She smiles innocently at the dog, whose old head is shaking with a slight tremor.

"Be quiet. You know very well the chicken coop was invaded, Ruby." Tomboy slumps down on the doormat. The exertion of the morning is catching up with her.

Ruby waits for her companion to settle in, then purrs, "Yes, I heard. It was all Francis and the chickens could talk about this morning." Ruby yawns again, her back arching gracefully over the seat of the rocking chair.

"What did they say?" Tomboy asks, alert with interest.

"One fox and two coyotes. The coyotes did most of the damage."

"So, they're working together. I knew we couldn't trust those foxes."

"Not necessarily. Maybe the fox was tricked."

Tomboy cocks her head to consider this new idea.

She has never really liked the foxes, but then again, they've been living side by side for years without a disturbance to the treaty—until now. And she had smelled the scent of coyotes outside the hen house and then again by the bear carcass. The fox she saw this morning wasn't an adult fox, but rather one of the kits from Pennyroyal and Moon's most recent litter. It was possible that something underhanded was afoot, and the foxes were caught in a deadly game of cunning.

Still, the treaty had been broken, and Tomboy was the kind of animal that lived by a strict code of immutable ethics. Most farm dogs are that way, as a matter of fact.

"The master bought traps. Either way, by the end of the week, the chickens will be safe." The dog thumps her tail on the porch and rests her tired head on her paws. Ruby regards the black Lab, noticing her graying muzzle and cloudy eyes. She hops down from her perch next to Tomboy, who is panting heavily in the oppressive heat.

"You need to find out what's going on, Tomboy, and warn the foxes if this is not of their doing," Ruby states matter-of-factly. Tomboy turns her eyes to look at her oldest, most infuriating friend. The cat has settled down into a seated position on the porch, her orange and white tail tucked comfortably around her. She blinks slowly at Tomboy, then turns her head to watch a honeybee buzzing around Mrs. Reynolds's roses as though she has all the time in the world. The dog sighs heavily. Then, with a tremendous effort, rouses herself up and descends the front steps toward the dove hunting meadow.

When she gets to the fence line, Tomboy puts her nose to the ground, picking up traces of scent. She can smell the two coyotes and the fox from the chicken coop. The old dog's eyes narrow, and she growls softly at the thought of these three criminals invading her territory. Whatever may have happened with the fox, he has some explaining to do.

Usually, she doesn't travel beyond the fence without her master, especially now that she is getting up in years, but she is certain that Ruby won't let her off the hook with this one. Grunting, she shimmies beneath the fence rail and trots across the meadow to the fox den.

The heat and humidity cause flies to buzz around her head as she cuts her way through the tall grass. She remembers when she was just a puppy, following the farmer in the early morning light, clumsily bringing back the doves he had successfully shot. Many years have passed since then, and Tomboy thinks wistfully of the shady porch and her resting spot.

Abruptly, she stops. One of the coyotes is close by. Her ears twitch as she hears a rustling near the tree line, and she sniffs the air, determining from which direction the threat is coming. When she catches the scent a second time, she hunches down, a low, throaty growl flowing from her jaws. There, just inside the forest, stands a large, one-eyed coyote. He is standing over the fox from this morning. The kit is not moving.

Barking loudly, Tomboy lunges from out of the tall grass directly at the coyote. Startled, the wild animal looks up from the fox lying motionless at his feet. When he sees the old black Labrador speeding toward him, he hesitates a moment before scurrying back into the forest and the cover of trees.

Reaching the spot where the coyote stood, Tomboy stops. She barks into the woods for a few minutes, then, satisfied that the coyote has been cleared off, at least temporarily, she turns her attention to the unconscious fox kit lying on the ground. His brown fur blends into the color of the forest floor, so he looks almost like a shadow. Tomboy thinks for a moment. She turns back to the forest to scan the undergrowth for the coyote. When she is sure they are alone, she gently picks the immobilized kit up in her mouth and travels on toward the fox den.

After enticing Ursa into a fight with the coyotes, Pennyroyal and Moon flee the duck pond, darting fast back through the darkness to the den. While on the way, they discuss seeing Shadow hurrying away from the pond with Mistletoe before the bear came crashing out of the hollow tree.

"What should we do?" Moon asks her mate, her voice full of trepidation for her children.

Without slowing his speed, Pennyroyal turns his head to her and says, "Mistletoe won't let anything happen to Shadow." His voice has a slight edge of anxiety, but otherwise Pennyroyal seems so confident that Moon believes him. She knows eventually the kits will grow up and leave the den to make lives of their own, but the beautiful vixen with the white stripe on her head can't help but worry for their safety.

The two dart through the woods to the fallen pine and its opening to their home. Once inside, Marigold pounces on them breathlessly, her usually authoritative composure shaken by panic.

"Mama! Daddy! Shadow left the den to follow you! I tried to stop him, but he left anyway!" As Pennyroyal speaks consoling words to Marigold, Moon goes over to Cricket, who is shivering with fear against the wall of the den.

"Are the coyotes going to get us?" she asks, nuzzling her head into her mother's soft belly.

"No, darling. Your father and I won't let them," Moon replies, feeling helpless. Her thoughts instantly turn to Shadow, and she wants to find him, but she trusts that Pennyroyal knows what he is talking about regarding the kit. Looking at her mate, Pennyroyal catches her gaze. He is listening silently to Marigold's prattling.

He interrupts her, saying, "Marigold, I know you feel like a failure, but I need you to stand sentry at the mouth of the den and look out for your brothers." Trotting over to where Moon is nursing Cricket, he continues, "Dawn will be here soon. I'm going back to the duck pond to see if I can find Ursa. I need to explain..." Pennyroyal's voice trails off, though a shadow of guilt hangs over his head. Moon's lips part slightly, but she says nothing—she simply watches as the king of foxes springs up the tunnel and out of the den, his tail like a torch in the dark.

Pennyroyal cuts through the night like a quick blade. Eventually, he arrives at the edge of the pond, where earlier he roused the angry bear from her hiding place. There are no ducks on the water, and everything is mysteriously quiet. The fox traces the path of the fight through the tall grass surrounding the pond. As he follows the trail of broken stems and cattails, he searches for any scent of Shadow, but the air is heavy with the musty smell of the bear and the sharper scent of blood.

Combing his way over the area, Pennyroyal hears a raspy, menacing growl coming from a dark patch of grass off to the side from where he stands. The fox freezes, his black nose testing the air.

The growl stops, and a faint voice whispers, "It's all over for you," followed by a hiss of laughter. Pennyroyal furrows his brow. He can smell that one of the coyotes is hiding in the tall grass, wounded, but he can't tell how badly. Judging by the sound of the voice, it's Nettle. He doesn't move a muscle. Nettle is dangerous, and if wounded, she is even more so.

He looks in the direction of the voice, and replies, "Good evening, Nettle. Please, tell me where you hurt. I can help you," Pennyroyal answers, although he can feel his courage failing at the thought of trying to assist her, should she let him, which he doubts.

"Save it, Pennyroyal. I'm as good as dead," she snaps, emerging on three legs from the tall grass at Pennyroyal's side. He looks at her, an ugly, painful smile stretched across her face. She lunges for him but collapses when she tries to put weight on her left hind foot. Her leg is broken.

"Nettle, there's a way to fix this," he says, breathing quickly. The fox knows that Thorn's mate is deadly, and yet he can't bear to watch her suffer, still attempting to fight. Something like admiration possesses him momentarily, but her next words bring him back to reality.

"He'll kill you, you know," she says, panting heavily into the broken grass beneath her struggling paws. She begins to laugh again, and the sound is like water freezing. "He'll tear you into tiny pieces. You're as good as dead too, fox," she spits the last word out of her mouth like poison.

"Not yet," he remarks, looking down on the indignant creature at his feet. All at once, a shot rings out in the direction of the farmhouse. Judging that mischief is afoot and the farmer is awake and has his gun, Pennyroyal takes one last look at Nettle and speeds back toward the den.

When he arrives, he finds Marigold sleeping from sheer exhaustion at the opening of the tunnel. Her eyes blink open slowly, but when she sees Pennyroyal, she stands up, stiff-backed and alert. Pennyroyal nods gravely at her, and going into the den, notices that Mistletoe and Shadow have not returned. Moon raises her head when her mate enters the dark room, their eyes shining dimly.

"Nettle's leg is broken," Pennyroyal instructs his mate over Cricket's snoring head. "I told her I could help. I don't know what I would have done, but I wanted to reassure her. She was still as vicious as ever." Pennyroyal tells her about the threats Nettle made and the gunshot near the farm.

"We heard it too," Moon says. She cuddles closer to Cricket. "I hope Mistletoe and Shadow are okay," she says softly, and Pennyroyal licks her kindly on the muzzle. Marigold has come back down the tunnel into the main room of the den, and the four foxes curl up together and sleep. At midday, none of them make so much as a peep until Moon hears Francis calling to her from the mouth of the den. Rising to her feet without waking her family, she ascends the tunnel leading out of the den and blinks in the bright sunshine.

"What is it, Francis?" she asks the raven after her eyes have adjusted to the brightness of the day.

"Coyotes destroyed the hen house last night, ma'am. And made off with two of the chickens. Your son was with them," he says, turning his head to look at her with his beady amber eye. When she hears this, Moon leaps on the black bird, pinning him to the ground with her forepaws.

"Who was it? Was it Mistletoe?" she begs the bird, who is coughing hysterically under her weight. Releasing him, he flutters up, combing his beak through his wings prudishly, as though she upset his outfit.

"No, ma'am. It was Shadow," he replies, still preening. Moon gasps. At that very moment, Tomboy trots up to the den where the bird and the fox are conversing and drops the limp body of Shadow from her mouth to the ground.

Chapter 14

BURNING MAGIC

Mistletoe's thoughts turn to Shadow as he and Ahwi walk silently away from the duck pond and into the forest. The vision in the pool this morning has alarmed him, and he is burning with questions about the coyotes and his brother, but he can do nothing other than what he has come here to do, and that is follow the stag.

Now that they are together, neither speaks. As they walk, Mistletoe occasionally looks up at the great head of the stag. The stars are shining brightly, and to the fox it looks as though the buck's antlers are hung with diamonds.

When they reach Big Creek, Ahwi stops and, looking down for a moment at Mistletoe, leaps from one embankment to the other. Looking after him,

Mistletoe scrambles down into the watery trench and climbs up the other side. When he reaches the top, he sees Ahwi galloping away into the darkness of the trees. Mistletoe races to keep up with the buck, ignoring the snapping branches in his face and roots twisting up to stumble him.

The red fox hears drumbeats coming from deep within the forest. They keep time with the pounding of his heart, and he scrambles along as though he is in a waking dream. The trees are like spies in the night, watching the two figures darting between them. From somewhere overhead, an owl hoots as if he is warning, "Turn back! Turn back!" But Mistletoe keeps pressing on.

The buck leaps majestically through the darkness, and soon the panting fox can hardly keep up with him. After a few more minutes, Ahwi has disappeared ahead of Mistletoe. The drums are louder than ever, and the bewildered fox stops, gauging his surroundings. From up ahead, he sees a flickering light, and following it, soon comes to a small clearing with a fire burning in the middle of it.

"Shadow!" Moon shouts, pushing Francis to the side as she bolts over to where the kit is lying. Tomboy backs off a few paces, then stops to watch the domestic scene unfolding in front of her. Moon drops down to her belly in the dirt so that she is eye level with her son. She licks and nuzzles him aggressively.

"A one-eyed coyote had attacked him when I found him," Tomboy declares, attempting to keep some authority in her trembling voice. "I believe he is just unconscious, but you better get him inside."

While Tomboy is talking, Pennyroyal ascends the mouth of the den, surveying the scene with an expression of surprise. He watches his mate struggling to revive his unresponsive son. He approaches and leans his narrow back against hers. She stops, looking at Pennyroyal with shining eyes.

"Where is Mistletoe?" he asks, turning to Francis. The disheveled bird has been hopping about peevishly, but when Pennyroyal addresses him, he stops and stands at attention.

"I don't know, sir. The hens only saw one fox," he says, scrutinizing the limp body of Shadow. Moon looks frantically toward her mate. Pennyroyal's face changes from a look of shock to one of determination.

"Francis, go and find him," the leader of the foxes orders the bird. Instantly, the black form of the raven rises into the sunlight, eclipsing the animals momentarily beneath his wings before flying off into the tree line of the forest. "Moon, take Shadow into the den." He stands aside as his mate picks the unconscious kit up by his neck scruff and disappears into the dark opening of the tunnel. Turning to Tomboy, the two animals eye each other suspiciously. Finally, the old Lab breaks the silence between them.

"I know about the coyotes. Tell me, Pennyroyal, are you working with them?"

"No," Pennyroyal answers gruffly.

"Then why was Shadow in the chicken coop with two other coyotes?" Tomboy narrows her eyes, determined to suss out the problem.

"I don't know," Pennyroyal replies, and a hint of desperation enters his voice as he says it. Shaking himself to calm his nerves, the fox relates the story to Tomboy of how Thorn approached him, and how he devised the plan to rouse Ursa into attacking the coyotes.

"Why didn't you trust me?" The old dog retorts, her cloudy eyes full of reproach. Pennyroyal swallows hard.

"I'm sorry," he mumbles quietly.

"Pennyroyal, you can't stay here," Tomboy begins, her head shaking slightly. "The farmer is setting traps for you and the coyotes tonight. It won't be safe to hunt." The fox starts at the mention of the traps but says nothing. He simply nods his head at Tomboy, who has turned away and is heading for home.

Mistletoe slinks into the clearing, his red face illuminated by the firelight. The drums have stopped, and he can hear the crackling of the wood on the fire. A hooded figure sits just outside the dancing flames. His face is obscured in shadows, but the fox can see that his long fingers hold a stick he is using to push the logs and stoke the fire. The stranger is humming to himself and seems oblivious to the presence of the bewitched animal.

Mistletoe watches the seated figure for what seems like a long time. Eventually, the figure stands up. He is impossibly tall—a long cloak covers his body from head to toe. Only the figure's hands are visible to the fox, who is watching him transfixed from below. With his hands, the figure slowly draws back the hood of his cloak, revealing the large, antlered head of a stag.

The stranger is Ahwi.

At sundown, Farmer Reynolds whistles for Tomboy, who comes trotting up to him from her shady spot on the porch. After he feeds the cows and pigs and puts them to bed, he'll be ready to lay traps and burn the carcass of the bear. He has spent most of the afternoon rebuilding the interior of the chicken coop and tearing down the cornstalks the bear and coyotes damaged.

The conversation with Bill at the hardware store earlier that day has put the farmer in a different mindset regarding the traps. Initially, he had intended to lay the no-kill variety for the foxes, but if a pack of coyotes are scampering about, he reasons that the no-kill traps won't do him any good, since he'll just end up having to shoot the coyotes anyway. Better a dead fox or two if it means getting rid of a threat to the farmer's livestock.

The sun is melting into the trees that surround the duck pond. The farmer pauses to admire the brilliant red and orange of the sky before walking from the barn to the blue Ford.

"Gonna get a fire ready, girl," he tells Tomboy. The old dog looks up at him good-naturedly, and the farmer chuckles softly to himself. "Load up," he says, and she jumps into the passenger seat ahead of him.

The two drive out to the burn pit on the north-eastern edge of the farmer's property, just outside the tree line of the woods. Hopping out of the cab of the pickup, the man and his dog walk to the back of the truck. Farmer Reynolds drops the gate to the bed of the pickup and hauls out the fresh logs he put there just before leaving. Tossing them into the burn pit one after the other, he hauls until the blocks of cut wood fill the pit. He then proceeds to pour out diesel from a can onto the logs. He lights a match and flings it into the pit, standing back a little as the wood ignites and the fire builds.

Well after dusk, the stars are glimmering like fireflies in the night. The waning moon arcs a silver crescent in the sky, and the smoke from the fire roils darkly away from the glowing flames. When the heat has reached its most intense, the farmer walks back to the truck, and lifting the tarp from the bed of the pickup, begins to unload the body of the bear.

Ahwi, the stag-headed stranger, reaches for Mistletoe. Before the frightened animal can escape, Ahwi has him in his hands and is raising him above his antlered head. The drums have begun beating again, and Mistletoe's body becomes limp in the stranger's hands. Ahwi stands, his arms outstretched, for a long moment. Then, as the drums beat faster and more furiously, the cloaked stranger lowers his hands toward the fire.

Beneath the ground, Shadow whimpers fitfully in a fever dream. He has not awakened since Moon pulled him motionless into the den, and his muted cries frighten the other kits and alarm his parents. Exhausted, Marigold and Cricket have fallen asleep beside their helpless brother.

"What are we going to do?" Moon asks her mate, her quivery voice in a panic.

"We'll have to leave. The den is surrounded by traps. It's not safe here anymore." Pennyroyal tries to explain, but his grief gets the better of him and he chokes on the last word.

"We can't leave. Not while Shadow is still like this." Turning to the kits, their mother curls her body around her sleeping son, who is caught in a nightmare. Pennyroyal watches his protective mate, a flush of love momentarily quenching the flow of sadness in his heart.

"I can go out tonight and find us a safe passage into the forest," Pennyroyal says reassuringly.

"No. No. Thorn will be looking for you. I couldn't bear waiting for you," Moon says, shaking her head in the darkness. The white stripe on her brow glows faintly.

"We will find a way," Pennyroyal says, the old resolute tone entering his voice. He snuggles closer to Moon and the sleeping kits. The two fox parents continue whispering over the kits' heads, trying to devise a plan to keep them all safe. Unbeknownst to them, Marigold has awakened, and is listening to the rise and fall of their conversation in the warm den.

As Farmer Reynolds throws the bear carcass into the fiery pit, Ahwi, the stag-headed stranger, lowers Mistletoe into his own fire, which is now burning hotly with blue-green flames. The drumming has reached a fever pitch, and Mistletoe writhes as his body is consumed. Enormous streams of sparks shoot from the fire, and the fox flies out from the midst of the inferno, his tail a blaze of colors.

In another world, Marigold waits for her parents' voices to drift away into sleep. Very slowly, she rises to her feet, and without making a sound, squeezes out from the back of the den onto the fallen tree trunk and hastens in the direction of the farmhouse. A few moments later, Cricket emerges from the broken tree and tails after her sister.

Chapter 15
TRAPPED INNOCENCE

Dogwood remains by the duck pond for a long time after Ahwi came for Mistletoe, watching the stars and listening to the wind rustle through the cattails on the edge of the water. She has only known him for a day, but the beautiful vixen has already fallen in love with the young fox, and her head is clouded with worry for him. To distract herself, she sings a little song. Soon, the frogs have joined in, and the night is resplendent with music.

Deep in the night as I wait for my love,
Music is swelling, below and above.
Lost in the song of my fairy tale heart,
Though worlds are divided, we never will part.

She hums the tune to herself as the frogs take the melody and add their mellow bass. Dogwood looks overhead at the waning moon as a chill slides down her spine. She trusts Ahwi, but she cannot shake the feeling of dread that has overtaken her. Rising to her feet, she retreats from the duck pond.

Dogwood remembers waking up next to her first mate years ago. The world had just split, but the animals were still able to travel freely between them. Her mate had risen one morning and told her he was going to the other side.

"I will be back before you know it," he said, his cunning eyes smirking playfully at her. That was the last time Dogwood ever saw him. The chasm between worlds grew wider, and neither Dogwood nor any of the other animals left behind could go to the other side to look for him or the lost others.

Many, many years had passed, and Dogwood grew accustomed to being alone. She had Pansy and Thistle to keep her company, and she listened attentively when Ahwi told his stories by starlight about what was lost returning to them. But she never tried to fill the hole in her heart left by the disappearance of her first mate—it was simply too deep.

That is, until Mistletoe showed up. Something about the clumsiness of the young fox endeared him to her, and she watched with interest as he attempted to make heads or tails of what was happening around him. She hoped he didn't judge her for the strangeness of her world and its innocence. Fiercely protective, she had only agreed with Ahwi to bring the young, brave fox over when she was sure he would not hurt any of the creatures under her care.

Upon meeting him, her reservations had melted away, and she had started to feel feelings that she thought were long since buried and forgotten. He was like her first mate—both in appearance and tone, and she found her mood turning playful in his presence. She thought of Ahwi's promises, and the more time she spent with Mistletoe, the more she gave into the belief that he was her mate, returned to her in a different form.

Still, she does not want to frighten the new fox with her strange beliefs, and as Dogwood walks along, she wonders to herself if she overplayed her hand. Ahwi had said it was important that all the foxes in Mistletoe's world defeat the coyotes, but was it true that their lost loved ones would come back to them? For the vixen's part, this is too much for her to contemplate, and she rids herself of the thought by shaking her head vigorously.

Dogwood is walking west, in the direction of the forest, when she sees him, just outside the tree line. He is sitting erect, his black forepaws planted firmly in the red Alabama dirt, with his bushy tail wrapped around him. When he sees Dogwood, he breaks into a trot and comes and greets her.

"Hello. Walk with me," he requests. Something is very grave in his voice. The two walk side by side, their deep red hips touching as they travel.

"I have learned my magic," Mistletoe says, not looking at Dogwood. She takes a quick breath. He seems larger and more imposing than he did just earlier that evening. When he does turn to look at her, his eyes are old and wild.

"Tsula…" she breathes, her eyes bright with tears. Mistletoe ponders his companion for a moment, then continues.

"I know how to defeat the coyotes. I must return to my world and save my family."

"Then you can come back, through the tree. This world was made for us," the beautiful vixen cries, her voice full of love and heartbreak.

"No, Dogwood. I can't. Ahwi told me if I leave again through the portal, I will not be able to come back. I want you to come with me." At this, Mistletoe leans his head toward her until their muzzles are touching. The two animals breathe together, their eyes closed. When the two creatures release from their embrace, Dogwood hangs her head in sorrow.

"No, Mistletoe. I can't. The animals here depend on my magic, and I can't leave them. Just like you can't leave your family," she proclaims, and looks at him, her eyes now proud and defiant, "I can't leave mine."

Mistletoe is startled and backs away from Dogwood slightly. He had not expected her to want to stay, but now he feels he can't ask her to leave, so he doesn't press her.

"I will find a way to come back," he says, and his eyes are deadly serious. "This is America. I'm free to go where I want." And he licks her affectionately on the ear, smirking faintly.

Just then, Ahwi approaches from the forest, his antlers growing like great oak branches from his giant head.

"It is time," he says firmly to the two foxes lost in conversation. For the second time that night, Mistletoe begins to walk off with the stag—except this time, Dogwood races in front of the pair of animals, halting their progress.

"Wait," she interjects, addressing the buck. "You'll need help."

"Wait!" Cricket calls out to her sister Marigold, who is dashing quickly through the meadow toward the farmhouse. Skidding to a stop, Marigold waits long enough for the smaller fox to catch up with her, and then resumes running.

"What are we doing?" Cricket asks between breaths as she tries to keep up with her sister.

Marigold doesn't stop, but calls back over her shoulder, "It's my fault what happened to Shadow. Now traps surround the den. I have to find Tomboy and tell her that she has to make the farmer take the traps away. None of this would have happened if I had done my job."

Cricket can tell that her sister is crying. "No, Marigold! Mama and Daddy will take care of us. We have to go back!" Cricket attempts to catch her sister's tail in her mouth to stop her, but Marigold is too fast. Cricket stumbles and gets a mouthful of dirt for her troubles. Spewing out earth, she leaps to her feet to chase Marigold again, but the bigger fox is already a hundred yards away and prepares to cross the fence line.

"Marigold, stop!" Cricket cries out futilely. And then she hears it: a crack like a whip, the sound of a metal spring collapsing, and the anguished cry of her sister.

"Marigold!" Shadow shouts, suddenly awake. He had just been dreaming that his sister had been caught in a trap. Pennyroyal and Moon pull themselves out of their individual slumbers at the sound of their son's screams.

"Shadow! Shadow! You're awake," Moon exclaims breathlessly, overjoyed that her son has returned to consciousness.

"Moon! Marigold and Cricket are gone!" Pennyroyal calls out to his mate. The den is all commotion as Pennyroyal darts up the tunnel to the opening above ground, and seeing no one, flies back down to his family.

"Marigold," Shadow sobs, still caught in the trap of his nightmare. "She's dead!" He buries his head in his paws, trying to block out the horrible vision of his sister's lifeless body.

"There, there," Moon says consolingly, although her eyes are full of fear. Before she can speak to her mate, however, the three foxes hear a voice from outside the den.

"Come out, little foxes. Come out and play," Thorn jeers. Pennyroyal, Moon, and Shadow all freeze. The leader of the foxes had been certain the coyotes didn't know where the den was, but there was no mistaking the sinister voice now uttering those words. He turns to Moon and Shadow, willing them to be silent with his eyes. He walks back up to the tunnel, and bows his head, almost in a prayer. Then, slowly, he ascends the tunnel, coming out in the meadow to face his adversary.

Thorn smiles when he sees Pennyroyal emerging from the broken tree trunk. Behind him, Voodoo and Ghost stand, their heads lowered and their neck hair bristling, although they are silent. At their feet lie the broken bodies of Marigold and Cricket. Pennyroyal stares at his dead kits and looks back up at Thorn.

"You can't stay here, Thorn," Pennyroyal growls, his heart throbbing with fury. "The farmer knows you're here, and he's set traps and will shoot you if he sees you."

"The farmer?" Thorn snorts with disgust. "We could have handled him together, Pennyroyal, but you decided to try and trick us." He lowers his head, his one eye gleaming wickedly in the moonlight. "My mate is dead because of you," he snarls.

"No, Thorn, she isn't. She's injured—"

Thorn cuts Pennyroyal off with a roar. "She's dead!" He thunders, his face dark and malevolent. "I did it myself so that she wouldn't get shot by the farmer." His voice has dropped down to no louder than a whisper. "She was afraid of guns." He stares at the leader of the foxes, but then transforms his face with an evil smile. "An eye for an eye," He scoffs, nodding at the dead fox kits. "This one, your farmer's traps did. But that one," he says, motioning toward

Cricket, "was a nice little diversion for us." And he heckles again.

Thick clouds roll in, blinding the stars and casting everything under a dark shadow. The fox backs up toward the opening of the den, as though trying to hide it with his body. Thorn notices the movement, and snarls—a deep, menacing sound.

"You can't protect them, just like you couldn't protect these two." He looks back at Voodoo and Ghost, who kick the bodies of Cricket and Marigold forward in the dirt. "Three coyotes against three foxes—sound like fun to y'all?" He asks his offspring, who smile and pant in agreement. "Let's fight," he says, and Pennyroyal lowers his head, preparing to lunge.

Dogwood sniffs the ground, and uttering a soft yelp, calls out to her friends below the earth. Before long, two long-eared rabbits emerge from their den, rubbing the sleep out of their eyes.

"What is it?" They ask the vixen, then turn and see Ahwi and Mistletoe standing behind them.

"Mistletoe needs our help," she says to Pansy and Thistle, whose noses are twitching nervously. They look back at the fox and the stag, then back at Dogwood.

"We will help," they say, and together the five animals enter the forest.

As the night grows thicker and blacker, the foxes, rabbits, and stag eventually come to the old oak tree with the strange, head-like growth attached to it by a vine. The portal is open, and through it, Mistletoe can see into his world, so like this one, but full of danger. The animals hesitate outside the tree, unsure what to do next.

"Draw the storm." Dogwood directs the rabbits. Nodding, Pansy approaches the opening in the tree and begins thumping. Thistle stands a little way's off and thumps in unison with his mate. Overhead, the clouds build and roil. A strong wind blows through the trees, and soon, the sound of thunder rips through the sky. Through the portal, Mistletoe can see the first drops of rain fall on the grass on the other side.

"Keep going!" Dogwood shouts, and the rabbits thump the ground harder. On the other side of the portal, it has begun to rain more forcefully. When Mistletoe can see the flash of lightning coming from the other side, he enters the opening in the tree.

On the other side, an enormous thunderstorm rages.

Chapter 16
THE TUMULT AND THE FIGHT

"Mistletoe! I've been looking everywhere for you," Francis caws at the fox from his perch. It is very dark, and the momentous rain has caused the raven to take cover under the branches of the old oak tree. When he sees Mistletoe emerging from the tree's trunk, he wings his way to the ground to speak to him.

"The coyotes attacked Shadow, sir," the bird says, ducking his head beneath his black wing. "Tomboy brought him back to the den. Farmer Reynolds has laid traps all over the meadow." Francis hops over a puddle pooling in the grass. Rivulets of water form over the ground as the hard rain beats down on the red Alabama earth, drenching the animals. Mistletoe, however, seems unaffected.

"Where are the coyotes?" the fox calmly asks his beady-eyed companion. Francis attempts to hop over another puddle, and instead lands in the mud, his taloned feet squelching. Pulling himself free, he flaps his wings, taking to the air momentarily before coming to rest on Mistletoe's shoulder.

"The coyotes have been all over the forest, sir. I've been waiting here for you since the rain started. Last I saw, three coyotes were heading to the meadow." The black bird shakes himself vigorously, then flies away from the fox into the trees in the direction of the dove hunting meadow and the den beyond. Mistletoe immediately follows suit, rushing through the forest like a quick wind.

Thunder crashes through the night as Mistletoe flies through the woods to the meadow. When he reaches the boar pen, he narrowly misses a trap laid by one of the posts of the pen. The boars are under an eave built by the farmer to protect them from the rain, and their sad eyes peer out from the shadows. They remain silent in their confinement, watching the wet fox speed past them, twisting his body like a circus performer to avoid the deadly snap of the trap.

Upon reaching the meadow, Mistletoe slows to a trot. The air is heavy with sheets of rain, but the fox can still smell his enemy as the wind thrashes around him. The coyotes are very close to the den, and

Mistletoe doesn't want to alert them to his presence until he is ready to fight. The rain has turned his red coat black, and he skulks through the tall grass, no brighter than a shadow in the harrowing storm.

❧

Pennyroyal lunges at Thorn, who steps aside deftly, avoiding the attack. The rain falls, and the fox skids to a stop in the wet earth. Turning, he lunges again at the one-eyed coyote, who laughs again as the rain pelts his gray fur.

"Do you really think you can defeat me?" Thorn taunts the fox, who is scrabbling in the mud. Pennyroyal circles round the large predator a third time. Before he attacks, Pennyroyal spots the bodies of his two daughters lying motionless on the ground. Voodoo stands over them, her dagger-like teeth bared at their father. Ghost is nowhere. Pennyroyal looks back over his shoulder at the den and sees the young coyote's hindquarters disappear into the mouth of the tunnel that leads down to Moon and Shadow. He vaults at Thorn again, and this time, the coyote is not quick enough to step aside. Pennyroyal swipes with his left front paw and manages to make purchase on Thorn's face, his black claws scraping over the empty eye socket. The coyote howls in pain, and Pennyroyal rapidly descends under the broken tree trunk after Ghost.

Inside the den, Shadow and Moon huddle against the earthen wall furthest from the tunnel as Ghost enters, his gangly body awkward in the small space. Catching sight of his prey, the intruder growls.

"Run, Shadow," Moon whispers to her kit, and Shadow climbs out of the small space at the back of the den as fast as he can. When Ghost sees the fox kit trying to escape, he prepares to leap on him and Moon. However, Pennyroyal comes charging down the tunnel, smacking into Ghost as hard as he can and knocking the young coyote off his feet. The surprised animal skids into Moon, who braces herself for the impact. He rolls into her, and as she takes the opportunity to bite down hard on one of his toppled legs, Pennyroyal flies on top of him, digging at the coyote's fur with his claws and biting his muzzle. The three animals roll about the den together in a tumult of blood and scraps of fur.

When the struggle finally stops, Pennyroyal and Moon stand panting over the dead body of Ghost.

"Shadow!" Moon shouts at her mate, and the two foxes run together up the tunnel and out into the thunderstorm.

Above ground, the two foxes see Shadow scurrying in circles close to the den, trying to outpace Voodoo, who has abandoned guarding the bodies of Cricket and Marigold and is instead chasing the third fox kit, snapping at his heels and snarling fiercely. When Moon sees her daughters lying dead on the ground, the heavy rain drenching their limp forms, her eyes narrow, and with a movement like lightning, she pounces on Voodoo's back, landing her teeth firmly in the neck scruff of the startled coyote. Voodoo launches into a roll to try and dislodge the fox from her back, but Moon holds tight.

While Moon and Voodoo struggle together, Thorn emerges from the raining darkness, his face bloody from Pennyroyal's attack and his expression terrible. The two animals stare at each other from their standoff, and then Thorn rises into a leap, tackling Pennyroyal and bringing him to the ground.

Up ahead, Mistletoe views animals struggling in the darkness. The rain is coming down in sheets, and the fighting creatures cast strange shadows on the falling water. Mistletoe stops, then enters the midst of the battle.

Pennyroyal gasps, the wind knocked out of his lungs as Thorn stands on top of him, the coyote's claws digging into his flesh. His hind legs slip in the mud as he tries to gain his feet, but Thorn is too heavy and remains pressing him down. To his left, he can see Moon. She has lost her grip on Voodoo and is held in the same position as himself by the young, angry coyote.

"Did you really think you would win?" Thorn mutters to the fox, no longer laughing. His blood mixes with the rain, creating a black river streaming down his muzzle and dripping into Pennyroyal's eyes. He blinks away the dark droplets as Thorn leans his head toward him, preparing to make an end to the leader of the foxes. Voodoo lowers her head down simultaneously, her fangs poised to tear out Moon's soft throat.

At that very moment, a lightning bolt flashes overhead, illuminating the animals in their perilous conflict. In the middle stands Mistletoe. The fox appears larger than before, almost as big as Thorn—and his enormous, bushy tail is glowing with an iridescent light. Thorn, Pennyroyal, Voodoo, and Moon momentarily forget each other as they stare at him. When another flash of light crackles across the sky, the large fox shakes his shining tail and unfurls a fire bolt that he hurls at Voodoo, who is pinning his mother to the ground.

The fire bolt shoots straight at Voodoo, smacking her in the side and unseating her from the top of Moon. Scorched, the coyote flees, howling into the woods.

Thorn unlocks his jaws from Pennyroyal's neck, baring his teeth at the stranger.

"What have we here?" He growls, lowering his head. Mistletoe gives the one-eyed coyote a sidelong look, then throws another fireball at him, flinging it with his shining tail. Thorn manages to roll out of the way just in time for the flames to pass by and land sparkling in the mud, harmless. He looks back at Mistletoe quickly, then launches himself at the magical fox. Mistletoe rolls away just in time, quicker than lightning, and Thorn goes sprawling into a wide puddle. The fox's tail is trembling with fiery power, and he can feel its forceful magic building. He regains his feet, and swinging his tail back and forth, waits for the right moment to hurl another fireball at his adversary.

"Leave, Thorn. There is nothing for you here," Mistletoe states, his voice heavy and commanding. The coyote looks at the fox, and for a moment, something like acceptance radiates from his one good eye. But then the coyote throws his head back—a long, mournful howl flowing from his mouth.

"I will kill you first," he roars, flying at the fox, his razor teeth glinting like diamonds in the rain. Mistletoe dodges him and scurries toward the den. The faces of Pennyroyal, Moon, and Shadow watch him, their expressions one of shock. Only a moment has passed, but to the fighting animals, it feels like an eternity.

When Mistletoe reaches the den, he leaps onto the broken trunk of the pine tree. Turning, he can see

Thorn just below him, snapping at his feet and growling ferociously. Just then, Francis comes flying through the dark sheets of rain, his black wings flinging water as he rushes at the remaining coyote, lighting on his back to peck him forcefully on the head. Distracted, the coyote tries to shake off his new assailant. At that very moment, another ribbon of lightning explodes across the thundering sky. Mistletoe launches a flaming fire bolt at the one-eyed coyote, hitting him squarely in the face. Without hesitating, Mistletoe spins, his fiery tail crackling with heat, and he flings one last blazing fireball at the coyote, who collapses on the ground, dead.

During an Alabama summer, dawn comes early, gliding with gilded wings above the deep forests of Big Creek. As the early sun ascends the heavenly stairway in the sky, the storm that raged all night over Farmer Reynolds's property fades into a light, purifying rain.

"Where have you been?" Moon asks Mistletoe reproachfully, her red tail curled around the bodies of Cricket and Marigold protectively. Mistletoe swallows hard, bowing his head before the outraged vixen.

"I'm sorry, Mother," he sniffles, choking back a sob. The magic that burned within him seems to have washed away in the rain, and he appears smaller and more fragile than he did in the night. Still, Pennyroyal and Shadow approach him tentatively, as though at any moment, he may hurl a fire bolt at them. When they see the sadness welling in Mistletoe's eyes, they lose their fear and nuzzle him tenderly.

"Thank you, son," Pennyroyal says earnestly. He smiles at Mistletoe—a warm, forgiving smile that almost makes up for Moon's frosty greeting. The young fox locks eyes with his father, who smiles unwaveringly at his son. A few yards away, Francis perches on top of the lifeless body of Thorn and plunges his long black beak into the coyote's one good eye.

While the rain falls, Pennyroyal, Mistletoe, and Shadow work to drag the body of Ghost out of the den, leaving it to rest next to the body of Thorn. Moon hasn't budged from her protective huddle around the dead kits, and the other foxes don't bother her. When they have completed their task, brothers and father stop to catch their breath.

"What are we gonna do about Mama?" Shadow asks plaintively. Pennyroyal and Mistletoe exchange a furtive look.

The three turn to see Ahwi, the great stag, approaching Moon and the kits. Leaning his great antlered head down so he is at eye level with the weeping vixen, he utters, "Come with me, Moon. Time awaits."

Chapter 17
WHAT COMES AFTER

Moon climbs onto the great stag's head and nestles herself into the crook of his antlers. Pennyroyal places each of the lifeless kits next to their mother, and then watches as the buck raises his head and strides into the forest. Pennyroyal, Mistletoe, and Shadow all follow.

When they reach the ancient oak tree, Ahwi lowers his head, allowing Moon to disembark to the ground. Cricket and Marigold remain in his antlers, as though merely sleeping. The foxes look up at the buck, who is standing resolutely just outside the tree. Light is pouring through the forest along with the rain, illuminating everything in liquid sunshine.

The head-like vine has turned, and its face is very mournful as it regards the sad scene before it. The trunk of the tree opens slowly, and through it, Mistletoe can see the forest on the other side, although there is a veil of light separating this world from the next. On the other side, a beautiful vixen is standing by the tree, and she is singing. The song floats through the tree to where the foxes and stag stand, and they shift their feet nervously in the soft rain. She sings of life, and love, and loss. The music is beautiful, serene, and calms the animals waiting to see what the stag will do.

Very slowly, Ahwi plods to the tree, cradling Cricket and Marigold in his antlers. His watery footfalls fall in time to the vixen's music, and soon, he is within the tree. But instead of disappearing, the buck merely transports through the tree to the other side. When he reaches the vixen, he kneels, and allows her to gently remove the fox kits from his antlers. She lays them in the grass, their bodies bedewed with rain and sunlight.

"There, there," Dogwood says through the portal to Moon, who is weeping openly. "They are only sleeping." Her voice is warm and comforting, and Moon swallows her tears, her shining eyes transfixed on the beautiful vixen and the lifeless kits.

Dogwood nuzzles the bodies of the kits affectionately, and lying down next to them, sings,

We rise with the dawn

To worship the sun.
Her golden rays consume us
Until we are one.

As she sings, Cricket and Marigold stir, their black feet twitching as the music washes over them, bringing them back to life. Soon, they open their eyes, turn to Dogwood, and sing along, their childish voices echoing the melody. The three vixens tumble together in the wet grass, playing and rejoicing in the new day.

The foxes of Big Creek watch the scene unfurl in the mirror world, their eyes misty with tears. The rain has subsided, and the dawn strengthens into a bright Alabama June morning. Mistletoe approaches Moon, who has seated herself before the tree, watching through the gap her beloved kits come back to life and playing effortlessly on the other side.

"I'm sorry, Mother," he says again. This time, she turns to her elder son, a beautiful smile touching her face.

"I understand now why you went, Mistletoe," she says to him kindly. Her lovely eyes regard the young fox. He is not as big as he was during the coyote fight, but something older and wiser has altered him. Moon notices, although she says nothing. He seats himself beside his mother, and the two sit in silence for a long while. On the other side, Ahwi has lain down in the fresh grass, and Dogwood, Marigold, and Cricket are busy weaving flowers through his tremendous antlers.

"Who is that pretty little vixen?" Moon asks after a while. She has been watching Mistletoe from the corner of her eye, and she can see him following Dogwood's every movement with his eyes.

"She's…" and his voice trails off, unsure of how to continue the conversation. Moon looks at him, a knowing expression crossing her face.

"You'll find her again. Trust me." And leaning toward her son, she licks him tenderly on the ear. "I love you," she voices, before rising to her feet and rejoining Pennyroyal and Shadow, who have been watching from a distance.

Mistletoe remains where he is by the tree, watching the three foxes on the other side dance and play in the sunbeams. After a moment, Dogwood breaks away, trotting to the tree and settling into the grass in front of the portal. Both she and Mistletoe gaze at one another lovingly, but the veil of light prevents them from touching each other.

"Long time no see," Dogwood jokes, and Mistletoe smiles for the first time since leaving her.

"I miss you," he says, and Dogwood bows her head shyly.

"I love you, Mistletoe," she says quietly, almost to herself.

After a pause, the fox replies to his vixen, "I love you too." If animals could blush, the faces of these two lovers would be red with heat. Dogwood raises her head and stares deeply into the fox's eyes. Marigold and Cricket call for her, and she raises herself up slowly, never breaking eye contact with Mistletoe through the portal. After another moment, Dogwood turns back to the playing kits and leads them away into the forest.

Mistletoe watches his sisters and mate retreat into the thick woods until he can no longer see their red fur. Ahwi has left with the foxes on the other side, his antlers adorned with wildflowers. The trunk of the tree has begun to close, and Mistletoe rises to his black feet, as though waking from a beautiful dream. With one long last look at the tree and what lay beyond it, the flame-colored fox turns away, and quicker than lightning, darts into the forest and the new day.

www.ingramcontent.com/pod-product-compliance
Lightning Source LLC
LaVergne TN
LVHW020716110826
845149LV00012B/2289

9781964686004